Praise for Winston Groom and His Renowned Novels

FORREST GUMP

"Do yourself a favor and read *Forrest Gump*. It may be the funniest novel I have ever read."

—Larry King

"A *Huckleberry Finn*–type odyssey, complete with the humor-tempered irony and insight of Mark Twain. A rollicking satire, milking laughs from our sacred cows . . . As much fun as a box of chocolates, but far less fattening."

—Robert W. Conrad, *Pittsburgh Press*

GUMP & CO.

"A farcical romp through the '80s and '90s that skewers liberal and conservative sacred cows . . . Groom wisely focuses on Gump's inept involvement with real events. After all, how can anyone create funnier characters than those history has given us?"

—Don O'Briant, *Atlanta Journal-Constitution*

"If it is Forrest Gump you want, it is Forrest Gump you get. . . . The faux-naif tone, the perfect rhythm, the constant tension between the 'fool' narrator and the 'wise' writer—people love it, and rightly so."

—Robert Plunket, *The New York Times Book Review*

BETTER TIMES THAN THESE

"I believe *Better Times Than These* will stand as the great novel of the Vietnam War, the one they will read many years from now, after the passions of the day about it have softened, to know what it was like, for the young Americans who were there, and the America that sent them there."

— Willie Morris

"Let me enthuse. I didn't think, before I read *Better Times Than These,* that a conventional war story could do justice to Vietnam. . . . But Winston Groom's tragicomic first novel proves this assumption incorrect. For he has marshaled the familiar conventions of American war fiction . . . [and] fashioned them into a mirror of hell that leaves one awestruck."

— Christopher Lehmann-Haupt, *The New York Times*

GONE THE SUN

"Unforgettable . . . Groom has sliced through not only Southern life but modern-day America with the touch of a poetic surgeon."

— Wayne Greenhaw, *Atlanta Journal-Constitution*

"Two landscapes loom large in the work of Winston Groom, both of them green, both of them hothouses for chicanery and violence: Vietnam and the American South. . . . Groom once again deftly blends his two prime ingredients and serves up a tasty gumbo, a well-written and engrossing novel."

— Nicolas Proffett, *The Washington Post Book World*

AS SUMMERS DIE

"Reminiscent of William Faulkner . . . [A] defeat of . . . evil as sweet as Southern Comfort."
— Elizabeth Wheeler, *Los Angeles Times*

"A classic, palpable account of prejudice, the tyranny of class and the terror of the underdogs, much like *To Kill a Mockingbird.*"
— Nancy Webb Hatton, *Detroit News*

SHROUDS OF GLORY

"A fine synthesis of one of the most important, if overshadowed, military campaigns in American history."
— Greg Pierce, *The Washington Times*

"A page-turner . . . Groom puts his novelist's eye to searching out the telling detail and the colorful anecdote."
— Stephen W. Sears, *People*

Books by Winston Groom

As Summers Die
Better Times Than These
Conversations with the Enemy *(with Duncan Spencer)*
Forrest Gump
Gone the Sun
Gump & Co.
Gumpisms: The Wit and Wisdom of Forrest Gump
Only
Shrouds of Glory

WINSTON GROOM

Only

POCKET BOOKS
New York London Toronto Sydney Tokyo Singapore

This book is a work of fiction. Names, characters, places and incidents are products of the author's imagination or are used fictitiously. Any resemblance to actual events or locales or persons, living or dead, is entirely coincidental.

POCKET BOOKS, a division of Simon & Schuster Inc.
1230 Avenue of the Americas, New York, NY 10020

Copyright © 1984 by Winston Groom

ISBN: 0-671-52267-1

First Pocket Books printing July 1998

10 9 8 7 6 5 4 3 2 1

POCKET and colophon are registered trademarks of Simon & Schuster Inc.

Cover art by Dominick Finelle

Printed in the U.S.A.

to Fenwick—the "Big Fellow"

Only

One

⁓⁓⁓

GEORGE MARTIN, A BANKER, WAS SITTING IN HIS living room in a well-to-do suburb of Boston reading a local story in the newspaper headlined "Barking Dog Saves Family of Five." George had never owned a dog, or desired to, but he had a sudden flash of feeling, gentle as a feather's tickle, that it might be nice to have a dog. The feeling vanished as quickly as it came on; nevertheless, it was ironical.

His wife, Alice, watching the nightly news on television in an adjoining room, a little den with a fireplace and bookcases and a built-in bar, got up and shut the machine off. She stood in the doorway and interrupted George's reading.

"Sometimes I think I can't stand it anymore," Alice said weakly. "Bad news. All we ever hear is bad news!"

It was true that in that particular summer the world was in upheaval, the year marked with war,

1

riots, assassination and chaos. Most people had strong and sometimes violent opinions on a variety of subjects; some simply didn't know what to believe in any longer. Children sassed their parents and ran away from home and lived on drugs and loud music. Laughter seemed to have been replaced with a dry and frustrated battle between the "Us's" and "Thems." Politicians, as usual, continued their sonorous booming and posturing. *Divorce* and *son-of-a-bitch* had become household words. Such was the summer of nineteen hundred and sixty-eight.

This unwholesome atmosphere extended from the White House down to the meanest Arkansas hovel, from posh penthouses on Manhattan's upper East Side to Watts's lowest ghettos. Frozen somewhere on the fringe was the new and ungelled marriage of George and Alice who, all things considered, were doing a pretty good job of holding their lives together in Wimbeldon, Massachusetts.

"Mix us some martinis, and I'll help you drink them," George offered.

"Doesn't any of this bother you?" she asked plaintively.

"It's only television," he said, not looking up from the paper.

"It *isn't* just television," she said in exasperation. "Those are *real* pictures—*real* people!"

George let the paper drop into his lap and looked

2

up at her. He took off his tortoiseshell glasses and rubbed his eyes. Alice was a pretty girl, twenty-six years old, with long straight black hair and violet eyes. They had met in college, fallen in love but waited for marriage until George had established himself somewhat firmly as a junior trust officer in one of the city's larger banks. Through his careful money management they had been able to put aside enough to buy a quaint old historic townhouse; they had two cars, were friends with a lot of fashionable people and also owned a sailboat, thirty-one-foot-long, which they used almost every weekend, weather permitting.

"Well, what would you like me to do about it?" George asked.

Alice sat down on a stool in front of him and shook her head. "I don't know," she said, "I just thought maybe we should talk about it or something." She was twisting her hands, and he could feel the edge in her voice. The smell of lilacs and jasmine and trellised roses wafted into the room on a breeze from the brick-walled garden out in back. Shadows had settled softly over the trees and somewhere in the distance was the laughter of a child.

"You know," Alice said after a moment, "instead of going down to the boat tomorrow, maybe we could just take a ride in the country. Go up to that little inn in New Hampshire for lunch."

Something impulsive had driven Alice to that suggestion because she knew that Sundays were for sailing, and tomorrow promised to be an ideal day. But just now she wanted open land rather than the salted air of Cape Cod. She pictured rolling fields of grain and soft green forests with ferns and moss-covered rocks in clear brooks and winding country roads and the neatness of small farmhouses. Another impulse, subtler than the other, had also invaded her mind; she felt it somehow, but did not know what it was nor would she ever really be sure it actually existed, but she would have to wait for tomorrow to find it out.

Since life brings the things most dear mainly by chance, the man who schemes to make millions, and does it, at the same time cannot buy the love or respect of another living thing; that, he must earn, though there might be a certain amount of calculation attached to it. This, of course, is no news to anyone familiar with most religious teachings or with literature or, for that matter, to anyone who has ever tried to break a horse. But it is important in the case of George and Alice Martin, because although each knew it in their own way, they knew it only obliquely. They had been raised in a time and place where *who* you knew was as important as *what* you knew—a world that, coincidentally, was crumbling around them—but a world in which

4

appearances and position had to be maintained, no matter what. And so on a lovely early summer day in nineteen sixty-eight the elements of chance and calculation were on a collision course with the Martins' new green Volvo sedan. They ran out of gas.

"Well," George said wryly, "I guess we know what 'empty' means now."

"It means what it says," Alice replied sourly.

"My old Plymouth would run fifty miles on empty," George said.

"Well, we're going to have to *walk* fifty miles on empty unless somebody's got a filling station around here," she said. "Wasn't there one back there somewhere?"

"Quite a way," said George. He stood beside the car, watching the orange ball of sun disappear behind some low foothills in the distance. A field of chartreuse grain shoots waved from the roadside as far as the eye could see, but there was only the silence of open country. Alice got out of the car too.

"Well, should we start walking?" she asked.

"Yes, I suppose so. The question is, which way?"

"The filling station was back there."

"Four or five miles, maybe," George said. "I wasn't paying much attention."

"Obviously," Alice said. When he turned with a

frown she had a smile on her face. It foreclosed a sharp response.

"It's probably better if we just go to someone's house and ask to use the phone," George said. "I don't want to be stuck walking around all night."

"There was a house a few miles back," Alice said. "A big pretty place set on the side of a hill."

"Unless I miss my guess there's one closer than that," he said. "Probably up ahead. I'll bet the farmer who owns this grain field is just around that bend in the road up there."

"Do you think he'll have a phone?" Alice asked.

"Everybody has a phone," George said incredulously.

Alice peered at him with raised eyebrows. "Let's go," she said.

Naturally, the farmer had no phone. But he did have some gasoline in a big fifty-five-gallon drum, which he used to run his truck and a tractor so ancient-looking it might have been the first of its kind.

"Won't take but a minute," the farmer said. "I'll get you a gallon jug, and that ought to get you up to the station 'bout three miles ahead." They followed him behind the barn while he pumped the gas out with a hand pump that was attached to the top of the drum. "You from the city?" he asked.

"Boston," George said.

"Actually we live outside," Alice said. "Wimbeldon."

"My daughter went off to the city," the farmer said. "It's where she got the dog. Just comes back on weekends now."

"What dog?" George asked pleasantly. He saw no dog.

"Oh, she's around someplace, prob'ly inside with the pups." He nodded toward the barn entrance, continuing to squeeze out the gasoline.

Alice wandered around to the cavernous entrance to the barn. There, lying with its face on its paws in the cool of the dirt floor, was a huge shaggy black and white heap.

"Oh, George, come here!" Alice cried.

"That's Sarah," the farmer said, without looking up. George turned the corner of the barn just as the heap rose up and began waddling toward Alice, who had crouched down and was calling to it.

"Her name's Sarah," George said.

"Come here, Sarah," Alice cooed. "Isn't she adorable?"

"Amazing," George said. The thing looked like a bear, he thought, but that wasn't what he said. "It looks like a yak without horns" was what he said. He felt like being witty.

When Alice reached out her arms as Sarah approached, there came a cacaphony of tiny yelps and whines from one of the stalls. The big dog turned and looked back for a moment, then continued toward Alice. The farmer appeared suddenly in the doorway, back-lit in the glow of sunset, the gasoline jug in his hand.

"Them's the puppies," he said happily. "Whelped her about seven weeks ago. Cute little dickenses, I reckon."

"What kind of dog is this again?" George said. "I've seen . . ."

"Sheepdog," said the farmer. "Old English sheepdog. Never saw one up close myself till Jenny brung her home to drop that litter. Said she's gonna sell them pups and make some good money."

"Oh, let's see them," Alice said. She got up and walked to the door where the whining and yelping continued, and she peered inside. There on a bed of straw were close to a dozen tiny forms, fluffy and white with black saddles of fur around their heads and necks. Several lay in a pile, two or three wandered about, others begged at the gate; one lay alone in a corner.

"Open it up if you want," the farmer said.

Alice reached for the wooden latch and swung the gate wide, and the puppies wormed out in all directions like fingers of water on dry dusty ground. Sarah ambled over and most of them toddled to her and began sucking for milk, reaching as high as they could, for she did not lie down. A few others went helter-skelter inside the barn corridor, and one came straight for Alice. She picked him up in her arms.

"I don't believe it!" she said. "They're the cutest things I've ever seen." She handed the pup to George. "Look at their big paws," she cried.

"This one . . . he, she ah, *he,*" he said, after a quick examination, "looks like he's not hungry now."

"That one's kind of a loner," the farmer said. "Hard to believe, but after six or eight weeks you get to know them pretty well, considering they all look alike. That one, though, he's—well, the runt, I guess."

George put the puppy down. "Your daughter— what's she want for them?" he asked. Being a banker, George thought it important to know the value of as many given things as he could. He had meant no more than that. But immediately the farmer's eyes brightened.

"Two hun'rit fifty dollars," he said. "Lot of money for a dog, I reckon, but these are pretty expensive kinds of dogs. Kind of funny lookin', but they got a real good disposition. S'posed to be good with children. You got children?"

"No," George said. "Not yet."

"Prob'ly good watchdogs too," the farmer said. I wouldn't want to go barging onto anyone else's property and run into something like that," he said, nodding toward Sarah.

"Yep, two-hundred-and-fifty's a lot of money," George said, silently calculating it was about the amount of a good used jib for their boat. The puppy he had just put down went straight for Alice again, and she knelt down, stroking him behind the ears. She looked up at George pleadingly, her eyes large and hopeful, the way she always did when she wanted something but did not want to ask for it out loud. George's brow furrowed, and his lips pursed, and he looked away.

"Vet's s'posed to come by here in the afternoon tomorrow. Check out some of my cows and give them pups their shots too," the farmer said. "Then she's goin' to put an advertisement in the paper. Reckon she stands to make two, maybe three thousand on them pups. Not bad, huh?"

"Not bad at all," George said. "I guess they're purebred then?"

"As the driven snow," replied the farmer. "She's got all the papers up at the house. Dog was real good stock, I'm told. First-class line."

"Well," George said. "I guess we better get started . . ." He looked at Alice again, and she was playing with the puppy; it was nuzzling her fingers and trying to crawl into her lap.

"Why don't you let me ride you back in my truck?" the farmer asked.

"Oh no, we're just down the road, thanks. Alice, we'd better get going," George said. "I'll stop back and bring back the jug in a few minutes."

The farmer nodded and began shoving the puppies back into the stall as the two of them walked out into the dim light.

"Oh, George," Alice said, the pleading look still in her eyes.

"Uh-unh," he said.

"Why?"

"Look," he said wearily, "I know they were really cute, but we've got the boat and the new car and everything, and besides do you have any idea how much a pain it is to have a dog—especially a puppy—all the work it takes?"

"I'll do all the work," she immediately offered. "You wouldn't have to do a thing. I'll put papers down, and feed it and . . ."

"Alice . . ." George said, "un-uhn . . ."

"Please, I mean, we don't have children now, and . . ." She left the sentence unfinished, and they walked in silence down to the paved road and turned toward their car.

"It would be a serious decision," he said finally. "You know that puppy is going to grow up to be a great big dog and then . . ."

"But didn't you love the big dog? Sarah? She's gorgeous," Alice said. She suddenly reminded him of a ten-year-old child pumping her father for a party dress.

They came to their car, and George poured the gasoline in, screwed back the top and got inside and began working the accelerator. To his surprise the car started immediately. He drove back to the farmer's house and found him outside the barn, raking. The puppies and Sarah were no place in sight. George got out and took the gas out of the back seat. "Where do you want me to leave this?"

"Just set it down, I'll get to it in a minute," the farmer said.

"I'd sure like to pay you for the gas," George said.

"Oh, no, it's not enough to bother with. I get it cheap here anyway," said the farmer. "Farm gas— no tax."

"Well, thanks again," George said, extending his hand toward the farmer. He noticed that Alice had gotten out of the car and walked behind them into the barn, where she stood with a foot on the stable door, looking wistfully down into the stall.

"C'mon, honey, let's go," George said.

"In just a second."

He waited patiently beside the car for a few moments. The farmer went on with his raking.

"Alice," George called.

"Come here for a minute, I want you to see this," she said, not taking her eyes off the stable floor. George sighed, shook his head slowly and walked over and looked down. In the rear of the stall was Sarah lying on her side with the puppies suckling their evening meal. All except the runt, who was sitting alone directly in front of Alice, looking up at her with sorrowful eyes, its pink tongue hanging out just a little.

George looked at the puppy, and it looked back at

him and for a moment he felt a twinge of softening, then dismissed it.

"No," he said, quietly, but he said it firmly, too, putting his hand on Alice's shoulder and leading her from the barn toward the car. Neither said anything else for half an hour. As twilight turned to dark and with a newly filled tank from the country service station they drove the narrow road back toward the city. The dashlights on the Volvo glowed green, and George had turned on the radio and gentle sad music filled the car. After a while he turned it off, and as silence rolled in, the silence of the country with the purr of the engine, his eyes still on the road, George said very evenly, "Do you think we could teach him to sail?" Alice pounced across the seat with a hug that nearly threw them off into a drainage ditch before George could slow the car and turn it around—back toward the farm-house.

"The problem is," the farmer was saying nicely, "the vet's coming tomorrow to give them their shots. I don't know if she wants to sell them before that. And I reckon he needs a bath, too, to clean him up a little, after being in that barn."

"We have some vets in our neighborhood at home," said George. "I think it would be a lot easier to take him now instead of having to come all the way back up here."

"Dunno," said the farmer. "I mean, she said she

didn't want to start selling them till next week. She was gonna take out advertisements and all. . . ."

"Can you call and ask her?" Alice said.

"No phone," replied the farmer.

George rolled his eyes ruefully. "Tell you what," he said. "I'll write you a check right now. I'll leave our address and number, and she can send the papers along. You might just tell her that 'a bird in the hand's worth two in the bush.'"

"That it is," the farmer nodded, "that it is."

"Oh, thank you," Alice said, almost tearfully. "I'm, well, can I . . ."

"Sure, go ahead," the farmer shrugged. "We'll take care of things in here."

Alice was almost out of the door when the farmer stopped her. He got up and reached for a big flashlight on top of the icebox. "You'll need this," he said.

George and the farmer had transacted their business and stepped out the door when they saw the flashlight coming at them from the dark direction of the barn.

Alice had the beam pointed at the ground, bathing the puppy in its light as he tagged along beside her, bouncing and nipping.

"Don't they have tails?" George asked the farmer as they stood together on the porch. He had wondered about that before but forgot to ask. It was unlike George to forget a detail.

"Yep. They're born with 'em, but the vet bobbed 'em off after the first week. Ain't supposed to have tails, the daughter says. Never figured out why. Whoever heard of a dog without a tail?"

George nodded distantly and ominously, having just shelled out two hundred fifty dollars for a dog without a tail.

Two

~~~~~~

THE FIRST THING THE PUPPY DID WHEN HE GOT INTO the car was urinate on the front seat. George immediately snatched him up and put him in the back, but within moments he was scrambling between the seats to get up front again. They stopped at a country store and bought two copies of a local weekly newspaper, and Alice spread them on the floor beneath her feet and placed the puppy there. He seemed to like it, because there was an air vent down there, and the cool breeze ruffled his fur. Within minutes he was fast asleep.

"We didn't even ask what to feed him," Alice remembered.

"I guess we give him milk," George said. "You can take him to the vet tomorrow, and they can give you all the information. Shots too."

"Poor little thing," Alice said. "I'll bet he's going to be scared tonight, being taken away from his mother."

16

"For heaven's sake," George cried good-naturedly. "First you want to get the dog, now you're feeling sorry for it."

"Him," she said. "It's a *him*, We've got to name him too."

"How about Bowser?" George said.

"Oh, George—" She stopped herself. "How about . . . well, it ought to be something, well, something elegant or regal, like ah, Jeeves. Or Hamilton or Oscar . . ."

"You'd think we've just purchased ourselves a butler," George retorted. His eyes were still on the road. "Maybe we can get him to answer the door and serve cocktails." He was playing the role of long-suffering husband, and was rather enjoying it.

"How about Clarence!" Alice asked joyously.

"How about *Fang?*" George said.

"You're no fun," Alice sighed.

Two hours later they arrived home. George unlocked the door, and Alice waited outside to give the puppy a chance to do his business before taking him into the house. When she came in, carrying the puppy in her arms, George had already spread newspapers over the kitchen floor.

"He can stay in here tonight," he said. "I suppose we'll have to work something out about where to keep him until he's house-trained."

She put the puppy down, and he busied himself investigating the nooks and crannies of his new home. "We have some cream in the fridge," Alice said. She went to the cupboard and got out a small bowl.

"He seems to like it here well enough," George commented. The puppy toddled over to George's feet and rubbed against his leg.

"See," Alice said, "I knew you'd feel that way."

"Maybe we should warm the milk up a little bit," he offered.

"Good idea," Alice said. George took a pan from a rack and began pouring the cream into it and turned a burner on the stove to warm.

"I think we should get a box from up in the attic and put an old towel or something in it," Alice said, "and an alarm clock. I remember hearing somewhere that if you put an alarm clock next to a puppy it makes them go to sleep. It reminds them of their mother," she said warmly.

"What time should we set the alarm for?" George asked.

She looked at him and frowned. "Really, George!"

"Hey, where'd he go?" George said suddenly. He looked around furtively, then went into the living room.

"He's just exploring his new home," Alice called out. "He'll want to do that for a few days. Oh, he's going to love it here," she sighed. She took the milk off the stove and began pouring it into the bowl.

"This can be *his* bowl," she chattered. "Of course,

when he gets bigger, he'll need a new one. We can get one for his food and one for water and have his name put on them . . . I think this is a good spot right here," she said, putting the bowl next to the stove. "He'll get used to . . ."

"Good grief!" came a cry from the living room.

"What is it?"

"Bring me one of those newspapers!"

"Did he . . ."

"He did."

"I'm coming," she said anxiously.

"Bring *two* newspapers."

Alice entered the room tentatively with the papers in her hand. George was standing in the middle of a Persian rug with the puppy squirming under his arm. George was perched on one leg, the other raised in the air behind him, like a flamingo.

"Did you . . ."

"I did," he said sourly.

"Oh, George. . . ."

What makes some things precious and others not, again, depends a lot on chance and circumstances, so that an aborigine who comes across a gemstone while digging for roots in the jungle might find it completely without value, though to a trained jewel merchant it might be the most wonderful thing in the world. That is of course, the simplest example. Where two or more higher forms of life are involved, the degree of preciousness depends in good measure on the sense of loss that would be felt if the other or others were suddenly taken away forever. Relationships of the heart grow in this way, and it is precisely that sense of fear or frailty, or uniqueness, that causes hearts to cement bonds that grow into love.

For George and Alice the beginnings of this phenomenon came with a telephone call from the farmer early the following morning. It got them both out of bed "with the chickens," as the saying goes, and caused great consternation.

"Mr. Martin," the farmer said edgily, "how is the dog?"

"Why, he's all right I guess," George said, rubbing his eyes. "He's asleep right by our bed. In a box. Why?"

"Well, I hate to tell you this," said the farmer, "but, well, the other puppies they're . . . they're all dead."

"Dead?" George said, uncomprehendingly.

"Every one," said the farmer. He sounded like he was choking up. "You see, yesterday afternoon, it was before you came, there was a lot of those big horseflies around the barn. And you know how puppies are, they make a mess and everything, and there was so many horseflies in that stall that I . . . well, I sprayed insecticide in there, just around the edges of the stall, you see, thinking that it would help keep the flies away. I do it with the cattle . . ." He paused for a moment. George sat up in bed and looked at the pup's box. He could not see anything except for his tiny rump, but he was seemingly fast asleep.

"And?" George said.

"Well, I guess the puppies, they must have licked off the flyspray," the farmer said hesitantly. "And they're such little things. It, it . . ." he did not finish the sentence. "And Sarah too," he said.

"I'm really sorry," George offered. He sat up on the side of the bed. "Do you think . . ."

"I don't know, Mr. Martin, but if I was you, I'd get that puppy to the veterinarian as quick as you can. He wasn't there all night, but he probably got into some of it."

"Listen, thanks for calling," George said hurriedly. A rush of panic seized his chest. Alice was sitting up, too, her eyes wide and anxious. "I think you're right. And I'd better move quickly." He hung up the phone and got out of bed.

"What is it?" Alice asked.

"Problem maybe." George went to the box and lifted the puppy out of it. He seemed deep in sleep, and his head lolled when George picked him up. But he was alive. George put him on the floor, and he toddled a few steps and then sat down. George relayed the farmer's conversation to Alice, and she bolted out of bed and began to dress.

"It's six-thirty in the morning," George said. "No vet's going to be open now."

"Well, we'd better call one and get him up," Alice said. There was fierce determination in her face.

The veterinarian they finally found kept his office in a two-story brick building that was somehow out of place from its dingy surroundings—warehouses, terminals and yards that were clustered around a railroad freight terminal on the outskirts of the village. George and Alice, with the puppy still in his box, were waiting in their car in front of the door when the vet, looking tired and irritable, arrived. But he was a young man with twinkling eyes and a reassuring smile. Peltz. They followed him as he unlocked the door and went inside to his examining room, where they were greeted by an almost indescribably grizzled figure in a soiled green smock, who peered at them from a doorway with a kind of nutty smirk on his face.

"Good morning, Dobie," Dr. Peltz said. "Dobie, this is Mr. and Mrs. Martin. Their dog might have got into some poison. Go get me some number three needles and a sponge."

The grizzled old man nodded at George and Alice and then floundered crablike out of the room. George noticed that he was missing several fingers on one hand.

"Dobie works for me," Peltz said. "Got pretty damaged in the First World War. Has a steel plate in his head or something. He acts kind of funny sometimes but he's real good with animals." George

22

cleared his throat, and Alice stroked the puppy's head.

The office was quiet except for the pathetic yelping of dogs and meowing of cats from somewhere in the distance. The vet gently lifted the puppy from the box and placed him on a long stainless-steel examining table as George reexplained the problem.

"You'd better call the farmer again and find out just what kind of insecticide he used," the vet said casually. He was peering into the puppy's eyes with a small flashlight.

"Yes. Do you have a phone?"

"At the front desk there's one."

George left the room but returned momentarily. "I forgot," he said desperately, "the farmer doesn't have a phone. He must have gone to somebody else's or to a pay phone to call us."

The vet nodded unhappily, looking down the puppy's throat. "Well, I've got a pretty good idea anyway. He's got some of it for sure. It's too late to pump the stomach. It's in his system by now, but with a little luck I think we can pull him through. The only problem is whether or not there's going to be any permanent damage."

Dobie reappeared with a box containing the needles and put them on a side table. He went over to the puppy and began to babble to him in a soothing kind of baby talk and the puppy stopped squirming and looked up at him.

"What kind of damage?" Alice asked nervously.

"Hard to say," the vet replied. He was feeling the puppy's stomach and he reached for a stethoscope. "Could be the internal organs, liver, spleen, kidneys—and you might as well know it—it could be the brain."

"How can you tell?" George asked.

"Have to wait and see," the vet said. "With the organs we ought to know something in, well, a week or two. The brain, sometimes it's more difficult. You can't give them tests like you can humans. You can only judge their reactions."

"You mean he might be . . . retarded?" George asked solemnly.

The doctor looked up and pulled the stethoscope from his ears and let it dangle around his neck. There was a quizzical look on his face, and his lips pursed. He glanced at the floor.

"Well, I've never thought of it that way, but yes, I guess in human terms that would be one way to put it."

"People say I'm retarded," Dobie volunteered, chucking the puppy under his chin. "So what? Don't mean nothin'."

"Oh! Oh!" Alice said. A tear welled up in her eye, and she reached out for the puppy's head and touched it gently. A pink tongue emerged and began to lick her hand. "Don't worry, baby," she cooed softly. "You're an orphan now, but we'll take care of you. No matter what."

"How do we tell if he's retarded?" George asked.

"Well, you have to measure their reactions," the vet said. "I mean, watch him closely, and if he starts to do things that are strange . . ."

"Like what?" Alice asked.

"Oh, I don't know—bump into things, howl, lie in dark corners, bite his tail. . . ."

"He doesn't have a tail," George pointed out.

The vet raised his eyebrows and nodded solemnly. Alice looked about to cry as she stroked the puppy affectionately. "An orphan," she sighed softly. "A poor little retarded orphan."

George shoved his hands into his pockets and stared dejectedly out the window. The vet had retrieved a sheet of paper—a form from a cabinet—and was writing on it.

"What's his name?" the vet asked.

"Doesn't have a name," George answered.

Alice was drying her eyes. "Poor little thing. He's the only one left now."

"Why don't we call him *Only*, then," George said, trying to lift the tension with a jest. The puppy suddenly began to scramble to his feet but could not stand on the slick steel examining table. His legs splayed out from under him, and he finally sank back down on his stomach, but his head was raised, and his tongue flickered out for something to lick, and his eyes had seemed to gain some sparkle.

"Only!" Alice cried out, stretching her arms toward him. She picked him up and cradled him. "That's what he is! Only!" she gushed.

"I was kidding," George said dismally.

The vet had stopped writing. He was observing the scene with an expression of mild disbelief.

"Only!" Alice cried out again.

"For heaven's sake, Alice, what kind of name is *Only?*"

"It's *his* name," she said wonderously.

"You can't call a dog that," George sputtered. He looked to the vet for support, but Dr. Peltz merely shrugged his shoulders.

"Why not?" Alice asked. "We can call him whatever we want." She turned to the vet. "Can't we?"

"Long as he'll answer to it," Dobie chimed in. I knew a cat once called Washboard. Got his tail clipped off by a man trimmin' a hedge. Finally went crazy and started bitin' people like a dog. Had to put him down." Dr. Peltz scowled and flexed his fingers impatiently.

"Only!" Alice declared dramatically. She rocked the puppy tenderly back and forth.

"Greatgodamighty," George mumbled.

The vet looked at George, who paused momentarily then gave a disgruntled nod and rolled his eyes skyward. Dr. Peltz wrote down the name on the office form. Afterward he gave them three vials containing pills and instructed them to bring the puppy back in three days or sooner if there were any peculiar symptoms. Then they left, Alice walking in front, carrying the carton with the puppy inside it.

George opened the door to the car for her, and she gently laid the box on the floor and got in.

"How would *you* like to be named Only?" he grumbled discontentedly before closing the door.

She peered up at him with a determined squint in her eyes.

"How would you like to be named Alice?" she retorted.

George shook his head and shut the door and walked around to the other side of the car. "Great-godamighty," he murmured again.

Three

~∽~

ALL THROUGH THAT SUMMER AND INTO THE AUTUMN they grew as a family, George, Alice—and Only.

After a few days of lethargic behavior, Only recuperated, or seemed to recuperate, from the effects of the deadly poison. It wasn't long then before he was weaned from milk and onto Puppy Chow, and this was spiced with tidbits from the table. At breakfast Alice always managed to cook an extra slice of bacon and another egg, and he also devoured leftovers from the supper table, and his coat began to lengthen and fluff out and shine, and, being the runt of the litter or not, Only began to grow. And grow.

On weekends they took him sailing. Ingeniously, they found an ideal place for him on the boat, down in the cabin out of the sun and away from the rocking and heeling decks that his paws could not grasp firmly. They put him in the little sink in the galley with a towel laid in it, and he was as snug as he was in his cardboard box, and the lapping of the waves and the rolling sea lulled him to sleep. In the car, he invariably wiggled his way into the spot on the floor at Alice's feet beneath the cool air vent, and rested his chin on the hump between the seats.

Otherwise, he was as protected as a child, and perhaps even more. When he grew steady-legged enough to outpace a walking human, he was put upon the leash. George bought a book on dog training and began to instruct Only "heel" and to "sit" at street corners. This he learned to do after not too much coaxing and scolding, and all seemed to be going well.

Except for the leash.

He knew the word "leash," and it was his greatest joy to hear it mentioned and then see the leash in the hands of Alice or George. But as soon as it was snapped onto his collar he would strain as mightily as he could against it, surging forward like a wave, even though he was not yet powerful enough to pull the person at the other end off balance. This though would come with time.

George, being a practical man, was dissatisfied with Only's progress on the leash and one day returned home with a shining metal chain, a "choker" collar it was called, which was slipped around Only's neck, so that whenever he began to pull it tightened like a hangman's noose, suspending his oxygen supply. Unfortunately, this medieval device had no appreciable effect on the straining and pulling. Only coughed and he sputtered and wheezed and strained again even harder. It wasn't that he was stupid. He was stubborn. This was evident, because once the leash was dropped, he ceased his straining. But whenever someone was at the other end of it, Only pulled and pulled. There was a world to see outside his garden, and he relished each moment of it, even at the price of being half-strangled.

Then one day Only was bitten on the nose by a poodle, and George decided it was time for more drastic measures.

They had been walking in the neighborhood a few blocks from the Martins' house when Only spied a wooden gate beside a brick townhouse. It had been a particularly exhilarating day for him. In the garden, the leaves had begun to fall, and there was a cooling northern wind in a sky filled with big billowing white clouds against a background of azure blue. In his garden, the sky was the only thing that really changed. Beyond the walls there were the sounds of the village, children at play, dogs barking, the occasional noise of an automobile or a conversation out of sight. But the sky was constantly shifting and moving in its striated colors of light, and the sun that rose and fell over the garden wall was out of sight when George got home and, leash in hand, came into the garden to get Only for his evening "constitutional."

On these occasions Only was beside himself with excitement. He had developed a curious way of demonstrating his enthusiasm by wagging his entire backside, for he had no tail, and by bouncing up and down like a kind of animated rubberband-ball; then he dashed back and forth in front of George until they got to the door, where the chain was slipped around Only's neck, and he inserted his nose in the doorway even as the door was being opened, and invariably, George had to drag him backward with the leash so that the door would not bash him in the face.

Once outside, Only was like a child who had just been let out of school early. There were wonderful smells and sounds and things to see, cracks and crevices to explore, places to leave his mark, new ground, grass, bushes and trees, and always the prospect of meeting another of his kind. But the real treat was the park.

The park was half-a-block of grassy playground, usually filled with children. There, the awful leash would be removed, and he could romp and run and furrow as he wished until George or Alice decided enough time had passed, and then it was again the leash and home.

But on this particular day George had taken a

slightly different route to the park. There was a house several blocks in another direction he had heard was for sale, and out of curiosity he wanted to get a look at it. Not that they had the money to buy it, for it was a larger and much more elegant house than theirs, but George always liked to keep up with such things; just in case, someday.

They were nearing the house when Only saw the gate, and, claws digging into the sidewalk, he plowed forward toward it with George hauling back on the leash. The poodle was behind the gate.

It was a large black poodle that looked relatively docile, but its tail was raised in the air, and it was staring directly at the approaching shaggy form. Only did not waver or wait. He lunged forward to the gate and stuck his round black nose between two of the slats. Without warning or sound the poodle bit it viciously, bit it square and hard, and Only jumped back with a yelp of pain and surprise and batted furiously at the large gash with his paws, wailing pitifully. It was only then that the poodle demonstrated the dimensions of its inhospitable disposition. It commenced a ferocious growling and barking that would probably have startled a tiger. George tried to console Only as best he could. He whipped out a handkerchief from his suit pocket and tenderly dabbed at the cut on his nose. Only whimpered pathetically, both from the hurt and from the indignity of the incident. He had just meant to make friends. It was his first experience with the realities of the world. It would not be his last.

For temporary measure, George tied the handkerchief around the nose as a makeshift bandage and took Only back home. When she saw what had happened, Alice was beside herself, and Only slunk over to her and buried his head in her lap while she soothed him. The handkerchief was removed, and it was obvious that medical attention was needed. Only was driven to Dr. Peltz who, with Dobie holding him down, scrubbed out the wound, injected the tender nose with a needleful of Novocain and sewed it up. He gave Only more shots also.

"The problem," George said, "is I just can't keep him from pulling at that leash. If I take the leash off, he seems to do what he's supposed to. He sits, he heels, he comes when I call him. But once the leash is on, it's impossible. He weighs nearly seventy pounds now. What happens when he gets bigger?"

"He's obstinate," said Dr. Peltz. "Some dogs get that way about certain things. These sheepdogs seem to have a particular antipathy for the leash. I've heard it before."

"Isn't there something that can be done?" George asked miserably.

"You could try an obedience school," the vet

suggested. "It's some trouble—but it might be worth it."

George looked at Only, who was lying on the examining table, his head resting on his paws, a fresh dressing on his nose. George's eyes narrowed, and he nodded and he gave Only a stern glare.

"Obedience school," he said. "Yes, I think that may be the answer."

"Obedience school," Dobie cackled. "Why don't you just enlist him in the Army? Make a guard dog out of him. He might even make sergeant one day."

Only raised his head slightly and shot a sidelong glance at George. For a moment George thought he saw a kind of determined frown cross Only's face. Defiance. George blinked his eyes. No, I must be imagining things, he thought.

From the beginning, the obedience school was a disaster. The class was run by a stout and firm-speaking Norwegian woman named Mrs. Ragner, who made it clear from the outset that she would brook no nonsense from dog or master, and she ran the school like some kind of Dickensian work-house.

Lateness was not tolerated, and stern lectures were delivered for tardiness. Alice of course was the one responsbile for bringing Only to the school, and Alice had never been on time in her life. One day toward the end of the first week, Mrs. Ragner began bawling Alice out for showing up ten minutes late.

"It simply will not do, Mrs. Martin, if you do not arrive on time with the animal. It disrupts the training and upsets the schedule. If it happens again, I will have to ask you to withdraw from the course."

Alice apologized, though it was against her principles since they were paying for the class, and that particular morning she had had to stop off to do an errand that took longer than she'd thought. During this speech, Only stood behind Alice with a hangdog look on his face.

He sensed the tension and the acrimony and for the first time in his life he felt like growling. He really wasn't quite sure how to do it. Somehow his consignment here seemed to be the result of being assaulted by the poodle, which he didn't consider his fault in the first place.

Furthermore, he did not much like the other dogs in his class. They were a bizarre assortment. Several small pugnosed and yappy creatures of Oriental extraction, a big chow of sour disposition, an Irish setter that seemed whiny and nervous, a Dalmatian named Clyde that he actually liked and an enormous Great Dane that terrified him. All were under the thumb of Mrs. Ragner.

They were taught to heel and to sit on command, but Only already knew how to do these. They were taught to lie down and to get up and to shake hands and to roll over and other silly things. They were also instructed on behavior at the end of the leash. In this, Only became incorrigible.

He simply would not do it. No amount of scolding, spanking with a newspaper, pulling or coaxing had any effect. The moment the leash was put around his neck, Only would struggle forward, towing whoever was behind him along. He dug his claws into the dirt, set his haunches and refused to obey.

After it became apparent that Only was a "problem dog," as Mrs. Ragner put it, he was made to stay afterward for special instruction. This also had no appreciable effect.

There was some indecipherable instinct that caused him to resist restraint of this kind. He yearned for freedom, to be able to walk about and to rush over and smell flowers or the deposits of other dogs.

He had been raised more like a human than a dog. True, he ate on the floor instead of at the table, and slept there too, instead of the bed, though sometimes he was allowed to do this also. He could watch the television with George and Alice if he wished, although he found the shows silly and unappealing, with one exception: he liked the Johnny Carson show because he liked Johnny Carson's face. It was a kind face, he thought, a happy face. Someday he wanted to meet the man.

One day, the leash business finally blew into a confrontation.

"Mrs. Martin," said Mrs. Ragner one day after a particularly difficult session, "I think it is obvious that you simply are not following through with the training your animal is getting here. I have given instructions about keeping him in line on the leash, but every day when he comes back he seems to get worse."

Alice was in no mood to be lectured. She had just received word from her distraught mother that her eighteen-year-old sister had run away from her first year at college and joined some kind of commune. She had picked up the laundry from the cleaners and found that they had put George's shirts in boxes instead of on hangers, and there was going to be hell to pay for that. The Volvo was running erratically, and as she was leaving the house, a credit card company had gotten an unpleasant man to phone up and threaten to sever their account even though she had mailed the check in a week before.

"Listen," Alice said. "Every afternoon I take him for a walk and every afternoon I do what you say, and every afternoon he pulls harder and harder. Also, I am tired of your speaking to me this way. Just who do you think you are, anyway?"

"I am the owner of this obedience school," Mrs. Ragner answered.

"Well, it's supposed to be an obedience school for

dogs, not humans," Alice replied, "and I will not be spoken to in this manner when I am paying you good money."

"Then you can leave and not come back," the stout woman said, and she turned on her heels and marched away.

Alice stood there for a moment, seething. Then she looked down at Only, who was facing in the opposite direction, gazing longingly at a stand of trees in the distance. The leash dangled limply from his neck, the end lying on the ground.

"Come on, Only," Alice said indignantly, "I've had enough of this!" He followed her to the car in his jaunty gait, head uplifted. He had won.

"Thrown out!" George cried wildly. "Thrown out!" Only was out in his garden watching gray wintery clouds sail overhead. A chill wind howled in the trees. He could hear the consternation even through the closed door.

"Whoever heard of a dog being thrown out of an obedience school! Seventy-five dollars down the drain! I could have bought a new anchor for that!"

"He wasn't thrown out," Alice said evenly, "I was—at least I guess you could put it that way."

"*You!*" George said. "Alice, for heaven's sake!"

"Look, George, that woman was a Nazi."

"I thought you said she was a Norwegian."

"Well, she acted like a Nazi," Alice said defensively. "She kept referring to Only as 'your animal.'"

"What's wrong with that?" George asked in exasperation.

"Well, he's not an *animal,*" Alice said.

"If he isn't, then what is he?" George asked quizzically.

"He's, he's . . . he's *Only.*" Alice began to sob.

"Greatgodamighty," George said.

Four

〜〜〜

THE NEW ENGLAND WINTER ARRIVED, BRUTAL AND harsh. Only's garden filled with ice and snow, and the leaves and vines and the fine aromas of autumn faded away, and he went out into it just occasionally—mostly when the weather was too inclement even for a walk—to take care of his needs, though by this time he had begun to develop a resistance toward doing *that* sort of thing in his own domain. But sometimes he simply *had* to be out of the house and he would paw at the garden door and would sit outside on the steps under the eaves or wander around, leaving paw prints in the snow, until the icy wind chilled him enough to scratch to come back inside.

Also that winter, he developed his first full coat of fur, and it was an awesome thing. The hair was long and thick, and the black saddle around his head and neck turned to dark gray—"Kerry blue" it was called. A huge leonine mane shagged down in bangs

40

over his eyes, so that at times only his large black nose was visible, and his feet developed bearlike fur that made them look enormous.

Days were short, and by late afternoon when George got home he and Alice sat by the fire in the den, George reading books and magazines about sailing and Alice studying a new kind of literature which had to do with women. At times they had arguments about this. Alice began drawing George into conversations that seemed to annoy him. Her tones became more and more shrill, and sometimes these discussions ended in a shouting match, and one of the two would then leave the room.

At first, when the shouting began, Only would invariably scratch at his door and go out to his garden, cold or not. Whatever it was, it distressed him, and since it was his first winter, he could only hope that the condition was not permanent and the days of warmth and clean ripe smells would somehow return.

But as the arguing went on, Only gradually assumed a different role. If, during an argument, Alice suddenly burst into tears and left the room, Only plodded gently upstairs behind her and, finding her lying on her bed weeping, he comforted her by nuzzling or just climbing up and lying beside her. Or if George stalked out into the big living room, where he stared unhappily out of the window, Only waited a while, then went to him to have his head petted and stroked, and sooner or later either Alice or

George went to the other, and the tones became
soothing, and in a matter of minutes things were
back on an even keel. Only began to see himself as
some sort of mediator, and he enjoyed this, for he
felt he had so little else to give.

He became the center of attention in the little
household. He continued to receive his breakfast
and supper-table scraps, and almost without fail on
Sundays there would be pot roast, and he always got
his share. He grew to love pot roast, even the carrots
in it, which did not taste as good as the meat or
potatoes or gravy sopped in leftover bread, but they
had a certain appealing flavor. The one thing he
absolutely refused to eat were the onions. One of the
great mysteries in his life was how a human could
eat an onion. Also, he usually received a long walk
on Sundays after the pot roast feast, with both
George and Alice taking turns being towed along on
the slippery sidewalks at the other end of his leash.
They even grew to joke about it. Sundays were
Only's favorite day.

During this harsh first winter something frighten-
ing happened.

George and Alice's nagging concern that the poison had somehow permanently affected Only came
to a crisis point when he began to behave erratically.
He started to bump into things. They began to
suspect his coordination was off.

At first, he would simply walk up to something, a
piece of furniture, a tree, an iron gate or a telephone

pole, and touch it lightly with his nose, then recoil. But as the winter deepened and he began to bound with abandon in the snow, sometimes he would really bash into something. He stumbled over curbs, missed doors, fell down stairs and finally he smacked square into a parked car, knocking himself flat with a yelp.

"I wonder if his eyesight was affected," George pondered.

"He doesn't seem to be able to see well out of the left side."

"Retarded," Alice said chokingly. "That's what Dr. Peltz said. It could be that he's retarded."

Otherwise, Only seemed all right; he did not howl or seek out dark corners, but after several weeks of running into things he was put into the car and transported to the office of the kindly vet.

Dr. Peltz and Dobie lifted Only onto the steel examining table, and the vet began his examination. He pricked Only's paw with a pin. He tapped his foreleg with a rubber hammer and he looked into his eyes with a light.

"What other signs does he show?" the vet asked.

"Nothing much," Alice answered. "Sometimes he barks for no reason we can think of, but that's about it."

"All dogs do that," he said casually. He was looking in Only's floppy ear with a mirror.

"Is he retarded?" Alice asked nervously.

"Hard to say," he said.

"Then what is it?" George asked.

"I know what it is," Dobie declared grandly. He went to a metal cabinet and retrieved a pair of large shears and handed them to Dr. Peltz, who looked at Dobie strangely for a moment, then at Only, and then nodded in agreement and seized the large shag of hair that covered Only's eyes and with a single clip sheared it off above his eyebrows.

"I believe that will solve the problem," he said. Dobie was hunched over, beaming into Only's bewildered face.

"You mean—" Alice started to say.

"Exactly," Peltz cut her off. "How well could you see if all your hair was hanging down over your eyes?"

"But the book we have says they're *supposed* to look like that," Alice said.

"Maybe," he said, "but if it boils down to a question of style or having your dog addle-witted because he keeps knocking into things, which would you choose?"

"Style, probably," George said wryly, looking at Alice.

"Maybe we could just brush it out of the way," Alice offered. George shoved his hands into his pockets and looked out the window. He knew that as soon as he went out to the desk to pay the bill, he would discover that it had just cost him twenty-five dollars to get a haircut for a dog.

* * *

Something else happened that winter that at first
was barely perceptible to Only, but it caused a
certain change of attitudes between George and
Alice and later a physical change in Alice herself.
Lying at night at the foot of their bed he would
occasionally have an opportunity to observe perplexing behavior between them. They would form a
kind of peculiar beast with two backs and make
disquieting utterances. At first Only was excited by
these displays and attempted to join them in the fun
of pouncing up on the bed and bounding up and
down, but he was quickly disabused of welcome and
immediately and unceremoniously removed from
the room and the door shut in his face. In the
hallway outside he would lie pressed against the
door, quixotic and uncomfortable, but sooner or
later the activity, whatever it was, ceased, and sleep
would come to them all.

But as that cruel and unforgiving winter drew to a
close it became apparent to Only that Alice's shape
had changed. She had developed a large belly and
sometimes hugged him tightly to it, and he sensed
that more was afoot than he was able to comprehend. Also Alice became mellow and sweet and she
sang songs and whistled happily as the snow thawed,
and she went out to work in his garden, digging,
planting flowers and pruning the bushes and shrubs
with shears, Sometimes she seemed so preoccupied
that Only began to worry. But also, she and George
did not fight much as she grew larger and larger.

By this time, Only was beginning to pick up a little more of the lingo George and Alice used. At first he had been limited to an appreciation of sounds like "no" or "bad dog" or "good dog" or "come here" or "leash" and he understood nuances of tones. Then more complex statements began to come to him, such as "Do you want to go for a walk?" or "Do you want a bone?" or "Come inside, Only." It had taken *him* a while to realize that "Only" was his name. At first he did not like it because it had a kind of funny ring. But, since there wasn't much he could do about it, he just got used to it, and after a while it didn't matter to him one way or the other.

Spring came slowly that year, but Only noticed its beginnings from his garden and was greatly relieved at this change in the weather. First the freezing snow was replaced with a damp chill and strong blustering winds that swirled and sucked at the corners of the brick walls of his little confine; but the days were noticeably longer, and the sun peeped over the top of the wall, and he could lie in its secure warmth for several hours a day and wait for his afternoon walk. The trees and shrubs began to bud, and the holes that Alice had dug in the ground soon began to sprout green shoots and then flower into sweet-smelling little plants.

A new trial developed that spring which perplexed Only no end and was the cause of even more conflict than the business with the leash. Observing Alice busily at work outside, Only, too, began to dig in his garden.

It began in a kind of random way and without much purpose, but one day something instinctive compelled Only to dig a hole. There was a fairly large spot of unbricked ground toward the end of his garden, and for some reason he could not fathom, he decided to claw at it. First he pawed at the ground and found it hard. Then he began using both paws, the long nails tearing at the winter-hardened dirt until he reached softer ground. The deeper he got, the more satisfactory the project became. He worked at it all afternoon, using not just his paws but his nose as well to root out the hole. By the end of the day, when Alice returned from some errand, he had excavated a pit nearly two feet deep and a foot and a half wide. Furthermore he was covered with dirt.

When Alice opened the door to the garden she shrieked in exasperation.

"Oh, Only!" she cried. "What are you doing!"

Only looked up at her black-faced and filthy, and a guilt-ridden twang of regret shivered through his heart. He shrank from this disapproval but could not understand the reason for it. After all, Alice had been digging in the garden day after day. She disappeared from the door and returned with a damp towel and began wiping off his snout. He assisted her by shaking mightily, as though he were wet from a dousing; this caused a shrill reaction and a firm slap to his hindquarters, and he retreated to the far end of the garden and sulked. Alice went back inside, and he was left to himself and that evening did not receive his walk and was brought in only for his meal.

But the digging instinct was with him then and continued and became obsessive whenever he received a bone from the supper table. Playing with bones became one of the joys in his life. His teeth were growing stronger and sometimes ached, and gnawing on a fresh bone was just about the most pleasurable thing he could imagine. Second was digging a hole and burying the bone, and third was digging it up again and gnawing on it some more. This, of course, did nothing to improve the appearance of the garden, at least so far as George and Alice were concerned.

"How do we stop him?" Alice said one afternoon, surveying the ever-increasing numbers of holes and excavations.

"It looks like Hiroshima," George said.

"Maybe we'd just better not give him any more bones," Alice said. "Just look at my crocus!"

And so for a while Only did not receive the bones from the table. He would sit after the meal, longing, waiting for his treat, but all bones were religiously placed in the big garbage can, and the lid fastened tight. One day he managed to knock the can down and paw the lid off and get his bones out and in the process strewed garbage from one end of the yard to the other. It was one of the happiest occasions of his life, but the spanking, reprobation and rejection this elicited when the crime was discovered caused Only to think twice before doing it again—which, of course, he eventually did—and after more such discipline he noticed one day that the garbage can had been fastened by some sort of strap to the wall of the house, and the top secured by latches, and that was the end of the garbage episode. Nevertheless, he continued to dig in the garden for old bones, the location of which he had forgotten, and also because it gave him something to do besides looking up at the sky. In time it occurred to George and Alice that they ought to give up on the garden this year.

"He'll grow out of it," George said. "Probably just a phase he's going through."

"Maybe we can teach him to dig where I want to plant something," she offered enthusiastically.

"He'd just dig it up again after you'd planted it."

"Maybe we could teach him to plant too. Give him a sense of purpose."

"He doesn't have any purpose," George said. "We probably should have named him Useless." He went back inside.

Only, lying with his head on his paws, stared off into the sky. He did not understand precisely the tenor of the discussion but he knew it was about him and he knew it was not good. Actually he thought the garden looked much improved. The mounds of dirt and the pockmarks gave it a kind of informal, causal appearance, like what he imagined the world beyond his own to be. Furthermore, it provided him some strange and indefinable feeling of accomplishment, a kind of control over destiny. In fact, Only was beginning to assert himself.

And then there was the business with the cat.

The cat had appeared one day in early spring out of nowhere, sitting on the top of the brick wall. Only had been let out into his garden one day and it took him a while to notice the cat. He had ambled out lethargically, still savoring the bacon scraps from breakfast and the taste of scrambled eggs and cereal and other things that had been mushed together in his bowl for a morning snack. The sun was shining brightly, and he perused the edges of his confines, testing the smells and fragrances on the breeze. Then he stood almost square in the middle of the garden trying to decide whether to find a place to lie in the sun or a place to begin a new excavation when out of the corner of his eye he saw the cat sitting on the wall, looking down at him.

Instantly he lunged upward.

The motivation for this was not out of hatred of cats, for he had never even seen a cat up close before; nor was it protection of his garden, though the cat had clearly violated his domain—if only in a peripheral way. No. The lunge was purely out of instinct and curiosity.

Just as with the poodle, he meant no harm, but the

cat arched immediately in a hostile and unfriendly posture, and Only felt a twinge of exhilaration that he could incite this behavior in another thing. He backed off a few steps and lunged again, and although the wall was nearly six feet high his paws had reached almost to the top of it, but the cat flew off to the other side and disappeared. Only began to bark. Up to this point he rarely barked, and certainly not incessantly. Sometimes he would let out a kind of deep "woof," when, as he did not have the human capacity for conversation, it was necessary to make some sort of sound just to let himself know he could do it; in this case it was, again, instinctive. And now there was one other thing for sure: He did not like the cat.

All through that spring and for years to come, the cat tormented Only. He never knew when it would appear. Some days the cat would not be on the wall at all; then without warning, he would look up and see it sitting there. It watched him with an evil and unforgiving eye. Occasionally it would stroll along the wall and change positions. The cat quickly learned that Only's vertical ability did not extend to the top of the wall and once knowing this, it assumed a tauntingly reassured attitude. At first, Only always made his lunges; then, realizing the limitations, barked. After a while he gave this up too, but he yearned for a time when the cat would relax its guard and come down on the ground where he could get his paws on it. This almost happened one day.

Only, drowsing and half-asleep in a warm morning sun opened one of his eyes slightly, and to his shivering dismay and delight, the cat had dropped silently into his garden and was sauntering across the bricks toward the other side. Only scrambled to his feet in a mad dash, bolting straight for the wretched source of his aggravation. Of course, the cat leaped dervish-like into the air and was comfortably watching him from the far wall of the garden by the time he had reached the spot where he had seen it in the first place. This antler-dance between Only and the cat had not been lost on Alice and George. From time to time they had observed it from inside.

"He just wants to make friends with it," Alice said.

"He'd be in for a surprise if he ever did," said George.

"It's driving him crazy," Alice said.

"So what?" George said smugly. "He's already retarded."

"He isn't retarded!" Alice protested. "He's just slow."

"That he is," George replied, "that he is."

Five

As the days became warmer the trees around Only's garden changed rapidly: Tiny green buds became broad leaves, and wonderful smells filled the air. Alice grew even larger around her middle, and George seemed happy as a salesman with a new and hungry customer. On weekends George would disappear during the day, returning grimy and exhausted, covered with dust and paint. After cleaning up and eating supper he would spend his evenings in the big leather chair poring over books and magazines. It was sailing time again, and the conversation between George and Alice was so much filled with talk of this that Only began to gain some sense of it, and the prospect excited him.

He had only been a tiny nipper on his sailing trips the previous summer, but from somewhere in his memory he recalled lying in the little galley sink, sleeping to the gentle rocking of the boat and the soft slap of the waves. And when Alice would sometimes bring him topside and cradle him in her arms he was content and secure as the seabreeze lifted the strange and salty smells of the ocean to tantalize his nostrils. When the weekend came for the first outing on the sailboat, Only had already sensed it and was aroused with joy and anticipation.

They piled into the Volvo with bags of groceries and other gear, and the conversation during the hour-long trip to the shore was animated and gay. Only was put into the backseat of the car with the window halfway let down so he could stick his head out and whiff the fresh fragrant breeze. After a while he tired of this and attempted to come forward between the seats into his old resting place on the floor beneath Alice's feet. But each time he tried he was rebuffed and sent back and once or twice he whimpered in discontent but when this did not produce the desired effect he settled down and went to sleep.

When he woke up, Only knew they had arrived at the shore: The smells of decaying sea creatures, sand and surf wafted atavistically in his mind. He bounded out of the car and roamed happily around the boatyard while George and Alice loaded the gear and stores onto the boat.

Working beneath the hull of a large yacht set up on a cradle was a paint-spattered man chipping away at barnacles. Only padded silently up to him and stuck his black bulbous nose between the man's legs.

This elicited a startled response from the man,

who dropped his tool and spun around savagely, causing Only to shrink back in fright; then a big grin came over the man's face.

"Well, I'll be doggone!" he said. "Look at you— haven't you growed up since the last time I seen you?" He squatted down and beckoned for Only to come to him, which he did, tentatively. Somehow he had known this man before, but couldn't place him. In fact, it was Burt, the operator of the boatyard, who remembered Only from when he was just a roly- poly furball the summer before. He petted Only and cuddled him and fluffed his fur.

"Lordy, ain't he a big' un?" Burt called to George, who was carrying a box of lines and tackle onto the pier.

"He's a moose, all right," George said.

Burt turned to Only and accepted a handshake from his enormous paw. "Well old sport, they're gonna make a seaman out of you yet, I guess."

The *Silkie* was a neat, trim-looking boat with a tall mast. It was sleek, wooden, polished and varnished and freshly painted and scrubbed and it lay beside a long pier on a small creek that entered a river that entered a bay that eventually entered the ocean. George had started the engine, which putted con- tentedly, and at last it came time to bring Only aboard. Alice summoned him, and George was waiting for him on the boat as Only made the short leap from the dock onto the deck. It seemed somehow much smaller to him than before, but he padded around investigating bow and stern. George seemed anxious and tense and even yelled at Only once when he began to paw at the freshly varnished cockpit. As George cast off, Alice, at George's instruction, took Only below, down into the old familiar cabin that was the scene of his earlier tranquil recollections. As he stepped clumsily down the narrow and slicked stairway he spied to his right the small stainless-steel sink in which he had wiled away many hours that first summer. Immediately, instead of continuing onto the cabin floor, Only put a leg up to the galley counter, hoisted himself onto it and attempted to lower his big hindquarters into the little sink.

Alice burst out laughing. "George, you have got to see this!" she cried.

"What?" George called impatiently. He seemed to be fumbling with many things in the cockpit outside, and Only, turning and looking out of the cabin, could see that the boat was now in motion.

"He's trying to get back into his sink," Alice said tenderly.

"Well, you'd better get him out of it," George said, "and come up here soon as you can. I need you to handle the tiller while I get up the sails."

"Only," Alice said sweetly, "come on. You're too big for that now. Here, let me help you down."

She put her arms under his front legs and tried to lift him out of the sink, but he was not in a cooperative mood. Something was very wrong here; this was what he remembered, the coolness of the little place where he rocked gently and slept in peace aboard the boat.

"Only, get down," Alice said a little impatiently herself now, but Only did not budge. This was *his* place, had been his place. He knew it. Remembered it . . .

"Alice!" George shouted, "I need you now!"

"Only!" she said, but he gave her a defiant look and turned away, still wedged ridiculously in the small receptacle.

Alice scowled at him but clambered topside. There seemed to be a great deal of to do: orders being shouted, responses in kind, and then suddenly the boat began to tip frighteningly as the wind filled the sails, and then the engine was shut off, and for a moment there was silence. Only, ensconced in his sink, turned again to look up through the companionway. He could see blue sky and feel motion and hear the lapping of water. But this was not as he had envisioned it at all. The sink wasn't really comfortable, and he had to brace himself constantly with his paws on the slippery surface of the galley counter to keep from falling out and onto the floor of the boat.

After what seemed an eternity, Alice reappeared in the doorway.

"He's still there," she said.

"Well, if he wants to sit there, let him," George responded from somewhere above and out of sight.

"This is crazy," Alice said.

"I told you he was retarded," George grumbled.

When the sailboat entered the river, the breeze picked up, and the boat began to heel dramatically to starboard, and Only found himself clawing desperately to keep himself in his peculiar posture. There came more shouting from above, and suddenly the boat heeled over in the other direction, and Only scrambled again to stay put. It was not fun! Moreover, it was scary and uncomfortable.

Finally George appeared in the doorway. Only turned and looked at him and saw George shaking his head and chuckling as he made his way into the cabin and stood facing Only with his hands on his hips.

"All right," he said, "enough is enough. You're going to fall out and get hurt or something. Now come on down from there let me help you." George put his hands under Only's front legs and began to lift, but Only resisted. The boat heeled farther in a freshening wind, and suddenly Only became terrified. He did not understand this discombobulating turn of his world. As George began to raise him out of the sink he did the first instinctive thing that came to his mind: He growled.

George let go immediately and stepped back,

braced against the cabin wall, and looked at him, an expression of disbelief on his face.

"Alice!" he shouted. "He growled at me!"

"Only!" Alice cried from the cockpit above. "He didn't!"

"He certainly did."

"Only!" she said again. Then there was a pause. "George, why don't you come take the helm and let me deal with it?" George scowled at Only and vanished upstairs, and in a few moments Alice reappeared.

"Now listen," she said. "You are just too big now to sit in that sink. You have outgrown it. I want you to come down this instant. Do you understand me!"

Only's eyes were wild with fright and hostility. Never had he found himself in such a perplexing situation. But then Alice soothed. "It's all right, good dog, just come down, and we'll go up topside. You can't sit down here like this all day long," she said. She reached out and began stroking his head and leaned over, her big belly touching the galley counter, and she kissed him on his black, wet nose.

Alice took him by his huge furry paws, and slowly, reluctantly, Only lifted himself out of the sink and stood unsteadily on the counter and then with Alice's help he got down to the floor of the cabin.

For a moment he looked back wistfully at the sink, then shook himself and followed her up the companionway into the cockpit.

* * *

Outside on deck it was fresh and cool and nice. The sun was warm and the sky cloudless, and they rolled before the wind as they left the choppier mouth of the river into the bay.

Only situated himself on the sole of the cockpit and rested his big shaggy head on Alice's feet and for a while went to sleep. The *Silkie* was on a gentle tack, the motion was calming, and things seemed to be going smoothly. Only drifted fitfully in and out of dreams of summer and his garden and the cat and security.

George and Alice had been talking quietly, and though he didn't realize it, Only had been the subject of their conversation.

"I've been thinking," George said. "What if he falls overboard?"

"Well, we . . . we go back and pick him up," Alice said absently. She was staring at a buoy in the distance.

"Isn't that simple," George said. "You just don't turn this boat around like it was a car. He's never been in water before and he'll probably sink like a stone with all that fur. We have to make a plan, and here's what it's going to be," he said, fiddling with the jib sheet, trimming it to the reaching wind. "If for some reason he goes over, I'm going to just go in behind him. Right away. Throw me a life cushion, and I'll get him in tow, and then you've got to stop the boat. Just let everything go—all the lines—and the sails will let out the air and then you push this

60

button here and start the engine and put this lever forward and turn around and come get us. Just remember, you've got to let everything go first, or the boat'll keep on sailing with the wind. But once it's freed, the engine will take over, and then you pull alongside—and, oh, make sure it's the leeward side, away from the wind, and put her in neutral, and the boat'll stop. Got it?"

"Got it," Alice said. She reached down and jousled Only's head, and he raised it up for a moment, then went soundly back to sleep, feeling warmed by the sun and cooled by the breeze and calmed by hearing the confident conversation, secure with his family.

The sea, of course, is subject to changes, some of them dramatic and egregious but in this case it was not so much a sea change itself as it was a new course George took when he put the boat on a new tack. Now the wind was almost straight upon them, and they were beating. The same gently rolling waves that had carried them out now began to assault the hull of the *Silkie,* pounding and tossing them about. For George it was exhilarating. He had trimmed in every inch of sail he could, and they were making fine way against the wind, driven as the saying went, with a "bone in her teeth," the spray and spume and raw power of hull and canvas against the elements of wind and water.

Alice had never liked this kind of sailing, for she

did not understand the dynamics of it nor the satisfaction that was gained from making one or two knots more speed, especially when it was so pleasant and gentle before. But she did appreciate George's enjoyment of it and the fact that if they were to return to where they had come from it was a necessity, and so they plowed onward, and the wind seemed to get stronger and heavier, and the boat heeled to her gunwales, and that was also a kind of scary thing.

When the boat made her tack, turning into the wind, Only was roused from his reverie, and, far more than Alice, the seemingly precarious imbalance of the little yacht frightened him. He was neither being held in anyone's arms nor safe and secure in his sink. He decided to get up and go below, thinking, wrongly, that it might somehow be different down there, but when he arose and lurched forward toward the companionway a heavy wave slapped the side of the boat and doused him with water. Then as he tried to make his way down the narrow entrance another wave threw the boat violently, and he lost his footing and fell pell-mell down the steps, landing in a painful heap on the hard teakwood floor. He stayed there for a long moment, lying on his belly, digging his claws into the impossibly hard wood. Each time he attempted to rise, another wave caused him to scratch and claw and splay out. It somehow reminded him of the stainless-steel examining table of Dr. Peltz.

"Alice," George said casually, I think you'd better see what he's up to down there. I don't want him scratching up the cabin sole. I just varnished it." Alice went to the doorway and saw Only lying in his fearful and helpless posture. She called his name, and he turned his head pathetically toward her.

"Oh, oh, poor thing!" she cried and scrambled down the companionway stairs and took him by the forepaws and then the hindquarters and helped him to his feet, and somehow managed to turn him around and coax him back up the stairs into the cockpit.

"Poor little thing," she said, "he was flat on the floor hanging on for dear life, He doesn't understand."

"He'll learn," George said, winching in the jib a little tighter. "Maybe we should have got a cat. Cats can hang on to things."

This sentence Only understood. It made him feel humiliated. He hunched forward, turned unsteadily and plopped down onto the cockpit floor again, facing forward. Maybe he should have been a cat, he thought sourly, at least he wouldn't have to have it lorded over him now.

In conversational vogue those days was a proposition known as Murphy's Law, which was formulated by some man whose name might or might not have been Murphy. It stated in simple terms: "Whatever can go wrong, will go wrong." Naturally, this law or maxim was intended to place people on the alert so that they would have a plan for unexpected contingencies. George, of course, as a yachtsman and a man of finances, had taken Murphy's Law directly into his bosom, which, of course, was why he had spoken with Alice about what to do if Only should fall overboard. Alice on the other hand, had a philosophy that embraced a kind of Divine Providence, or something roughly like it. Whatever the case, both were right that afternoon and both were partially wrong, which is usually the way things turn out. In the first instance, George was correct in assuming that trouble was, as it were, in the wind. Only woke up, got restless and stiff, decided to climb onto the cockpit seat beside Alice and coincidentally with a violent lurch of a wave against the boat he tumbled right out of the cockpit, through the lifelines and into the cold North Atlantic waters.

He came up, shocked, sputtering the salty water, disoriented and watching curiously as the little boat sailed on, leaving him bobbing in the ocean. Then suddenly he saw a flash of blue leave the boat as George, a small life cushion in hand, plunged off the stern, some distance ahead.

Except for the rain and his periodic baths and one time when he had waded into a stream chest-high, Only had never been exposed to water—and certainly not when he couldn't get his feet on anything below. There were a few terrifying seconds when he felt himself slipping under, got his mouth and nose unpleasantly inundated and his coat seemed like a great heavy sponge, but in his kicking and striking and thrashing he discovered the mysteries of swimming by the most expedient method possible—absolute necessity.

He began to paddle toward George, whom he could occasionally catch a glimpse of through the waves. The sea seemed vastly different from this perspective: The waves appeared enormous as they rolled across Only, dousing him under, then lifting him up. The *Silkie* was not in view when Only reached George, who had been swimming toward him and now extended an arm. George tried to get Only to put his paws on the life cushion, but it kept sinking and slipping, and Only found himself clawing at the water. George continually yelled furious instructions to Alice, whom Only glimpsed standing in the stern of the boat, yelling back.

With nightmare slowness, the boat began to turn until it was sideways to them, but it was very far off, and the sails began to flap violently, and its motion seemed to have stopped. There was further yelling from George, and Only sensed from the tone of it that something might be very wrong.

In fact, the boat had "gone into irons," meaning that the wind was now blowing dead into her, along both sides of the sails, and so was going nowhere. Alice was working frantically at the engine control panel, but to no avail. The engine would not start. George, of course, realized this, and it was the reason for his panicked yelling. He also realized several other things: that the water, even in early summer, was far colder than he had expected and that it was taking a toll on his endurance; also, that he was still dressed in his trousers, shirt, sweater, shoes, foul-weather jacket and that the little life cushion was not going to hold him up, especially with Only's bulk dragging them down.

Suddenly the *Silkie* seemed to tilt precariously and then righted itself and sailed toward them. George continued to yell and as the boat drew nearer his yelling became almost hysterical—for he saw that Alice was steering up on the windward side, and given the present sea conditions and speed, all six tons of the little yacht were bearing directly down on them and might not be able to be stopped in time. George seized Only by the neck and began to kick furiously out of the way just as the boat crashed past them. Clear of it, but still in trouble, he hollered a stream of things at Alice, received some curt reply, then he and Only watched, treading water, as the boat turned again, this time with a violent lurch of its big boom. Once more it roared past them, but there was a rope of some kind dragging in the water, and George seized it.

Without warning Only felt himself being dragged underwater. He was now being towed along like some kind of fishing lure. George had grabbed hold of a loosed jib sheet, but it was pulling them both beneath the water. After what seemed like a hatefully long time, Only felt himself released from George's grasp and bobbed to the surface, coughing and sputtering. He looked around, and George was gone. Then he saw the boat sailing off again, with George scrambling aboard, his legs disappearing into the cockpit. Only knew now that things would be all right. He began to paddle slowly behind, following the boat's erratic course. There was mad activity on deck as George ran forward and dropped the sails. They began to blow about wildly on the decks, and he rushed up and down, trying to rein them in and tie them down. Only could also see Alice at the tiller turning the boat again, this time under power, for Only could hear the chug of the engine.

Aboard the boat, things were chaotic. George did not want Alice in her pregnant condition to help him with the sails. He had discovered immediately that she had not been able to start the engine because she had pulled the choke button instead of pushing the starter. His first task was to get the motor going, which also took some time since it was flooded, and then get the sails down so they could go back for Only. To make things worse, as George had hauled himself back aboard, it came over him that when he had let go of Only, he might have gone down for the final time.

Alice, in the cockpit, was scanning the sea behind them. "I still don't see him!" she cried.

"Just keep looking," George shouted. "Don't take your eyes off the water. Look for the life cushion—I let it drop when I grabbed the jib sheet. He'll probably be somewhere near it.

"Oh, God!" Alice cried, near hysteria. "Oh please, God!"

The *Silkie* made a very wide, slow circle.

Paddling as fast as he could behind it, but far off—perhaps a hundred yards—Only watched as George made his way back to the stern, and Alice disappeared below and came up with binoculars. Slowly they both scanned the sea, but Only could tell, whenever a wave lifted him and the boat came back into view, that they were looking in the wrong direction. Somehow, though he could not know it at the time, during the wild scramble to get the engine started and the sails down, the boat had been turned around, so that where they both believed Only would be was, in fact, exactly in the opposite direction, and furthermore, he himself had moved a considerable distance, paddling after the boat.

"I see it!" Alice screamed.

"Where?" George shouted.

"Way over there, to port." She was pointing wildly, and the boat suddenly made a ninety-degree turn and headed straight away from Only, who continued to paddle along.

It was the little blue life cushion they had spotted. George used a boat pole to fish it out of the water as they both scanned intently all around it. But by now,

Only was farther away from them than he had ever been. He could occasionally see the boat from time to time, in the distance, bobbing up and down, then making another wide circle, but always farther south, and growing more distant. He knew they would never abandon him, but he also knew something had gone terribly wrong. He tried to bark once, but the sea filled his throat and caused him to choke. Also, it was getting darker, and the boat was harder to see. Only was getting tired and the water chilled him.

Aboard the *Silkie* a horrible unspeaking calmness had set in. Neither Alice nor George had raised the question openly, but each knew the search might now be futile.

"The current would obviously have carried him this way," George said. "Turn about five degrees starboard." In fact, he would have been correct if Only had stayed put, for the tide had been going out. But, of course, he had paddled against it in his effort to reach the boat and was far up course from where the two unhappy occupants of the *Silkie* were searching.

There was no telling how long he had been in the water at this point. Only had lost sense of practically everything, but he was driven by some inner will to catch up to the boat, which he could now barely see. Every so often he glimpsed a faint silhouette of the little yacht and heard the purr of its engine above the wind. Now and then, the beam of one of its search-lights appeared, but finally he lost sight of even this. Darkness had closed in completely and suddenly a cold, horrible panic clawed at his heart and shivered in his mind. He was alone with the waves and the whistling sea wind. All alone.

George had been the one to say it, though he saw Alice knew, too, for the tears were streaming down her cheeks as the beam of the searchlight flashed across her face. George had known it for some time, but had said nothing.

"I'm afraid it's no good" was the way he finally put it.

Alice did not reply. There was bitterness in her mouth and her eyes, but she was not sobbing.

"I know he's out there," she said. "Somewhere."

"Alice," George said tenderly, "It's been nearly three hours."

"Don't say it, please."

He moved the tiller gently and turned the bow of the *Silkie* toward the tiny lights dancing distantly on the shore.

"Can't we make one more sweep?" she pleaded.

"Of course we can," he said gently. "Of course we can." He was fighting back the tears himself.

"Oh damn!" she cried, "Oh damn!" and rushed sobbing down into the cabin.

George took a deep breath. He moved the search-light across the horizon again, but all was empty sea, great rolling waves in the blackness and an occasional sparkle of some luminous marine creature. "It's my fault," he said to himself. "I should have marked him, brought the boat about and just gone and fished him out. Or stayed with him. Or if I had just . . ." He let the thought drop off.

As he scanned again he felt something heavy and warm across his shoulders. Alice had come up with a blanket from below. He had nearly forgotten that he was still damp and shivering cold from his own dunking. She arranged the blanket around his body and hugged him tightly. He could feel her heaving, silent sobs on his back.

"I'm sorry, babe," he said. "I'm . . ."

"Let's don't talk," she said, "not for just a while."

George eased the tiller around a little until the bow again pointed toward the shore, and the *Silkie* slapped onward toward port. He lifted the blanket and took her by the arm and turned her toward him, bringing her beneath it. They held to each other in their sorrow and despair; the realization and the shock had still just begun to make its impact, and for now, it was simply inconsolable grief.

Six

〜〜〜

O<small>UT IN THE DARK OFFSHORE WATERS, O</small>NLY PADDLED
relentlessly. He had long since lost sight of the *Silkie*
and could catch only occasional shimmers of the far
distant lights on shore whenever a wave lifted him to
its crest. He was frightened and bewildered. There
must be some reason for this, he knew. Some
unfathomable cause he could not understand. When
George had jumped into the water Only realized he
was there to help him, and then when George had
grabbed him that last time, towed him under, then
released him and climbed back aboard the boat, all
of his instincts still had told him they would come
back and pick him up, and so he had paddled after
the boat, figuring they would stop and see him. . . .
But now, he was more confused than ever. There
was no boat in sight, and he was becoming very, very
tired, and the water continued to tug down on him
like a great weight.

If there was one thing he sensed about his predicament it was that they were not going to come and get him. He decided it would be best to go for the tiny lights ashore, for that was where the boat had been headed as it faded from his view, and the sea in all other directions exuded the darkness of midnights. It seemed that however hard he paddled, he got no closer; whenever he was lifted on a wave, it appeared that the lights ashore were the same.

As time passed a kind of satisfying numbness set in. He had been paddling for so long nothing seemed to matter. He had no real sense of death. He did have an instinctive sense of danger, but death was something he had not learned to comprehend. But his heart was big, and he paddled on, without heed to the enormous odds working against him. After a time—a long time—he began to notice the shore lights seemed larger. But then he could not be sure. Lights were human things and so were always subject to change without explanation. This, too, he knew. Still he paddled toward them.

He occupied himself from time to time with thoughts of pot roast, of the unpleasant cat in his garden—one day he would get at that cat, he promised—and of the garden itself, cratered and comfortable. He pictured himself seated by the fire on winter evenings with George and Alice reading and talking, and remembered how he would get up and walk over to one of them and his head would be patted and stroked, or how he would rub up against the big sofa. He recalled fondly the walks in the neighborhood, even with the terrible leash around his neck. The leash was another thing he could never really understand, for he yearned for the freedom to romp as he wanted, to smell what he wished, to chase whatever would run; yet he did appreciate, at least partially, that the leash was somehow a necessary thing, or George and Alice wouldn't have used it on him any more than they would have left him out here on the dark ocean this night. He did not even know he had failed obedience school, but he did know obedience was necessary so as not to get reprimands. As he paddled on, he considered reprimands too—those harshly spoken words that caused him to lower his backside and slink down, which, having no tail to draw between his legs, was his sole way of showing remorse.

Without warning, a new and fearful thing happened. He suddenly slipped under water and began to sink down.

At first he did not even realize it, until he sucked in a breath and got the horrible sea water instead of air. There was a long moment when something in his brain felt like relaxing and simply letting the water take him down into its darkness, and then another impulse, stronger, more powerful, caused him to fight the first and paw with all his might. He could not tell which way he was going; there seemed to be no up or down, and his eyes stung badly from the water, but somehow he broke the surface, and his heartbeat increased so much it was the strongest sensation he had, even above the sound of waves and wind. This happened several times more, but each time he resisted the siren's call to sink down and end all the pain and exhaustion. And also, each time it became easier to fight on. He finally got past caring about pain and fatigue, and time became totally immeasurable.

Once when a wave tossed him to its peak he noticed a faint aura of light in the sky. As he struggled onward, Only began to make out shapes of houses ahead of him, and closer, dark, black shapes, too, and then the grayness of dawn gave way to a pinkness in the sky, and overhead he saw white birds circling and diving.

He struggled on and finally got a brief view of a long stretch of whiteness and also heard a roar: steady, then at intervals, and the waves that had seemed so chaotic soon began to take different shapes and forms.

Then he saw a human figure on the beach. It might have been George, but from this distance and with only his head above water he couldn't tell, and the figure was periodically lost behind the waves and seemed to be moving away from him. He changed course and followed it along, and finally tried a bark. The figure stopped for a moment and scanned the ocean toward Only, then started trudging on again. Only let out another bark, this time coming up again with a snoutful of water, and he paddled with all his might to intercept the figure. Suddenly he found himself propelled forward in a rush as a wave lifted him, then passed under him, and as it did he felt something beneath his feet; then just as suddenly a huge mountain of water crashed over his head and sent him tumbling, terrified, head-over-paws, into a pebbly kind of mush. As he struggled to gain footing another wall of water smashed into him, and then, in the confusion, he felt himself being hauled toward the beach, out of the water.

It was the human, but it wasn't George. It was an older, kind-looking man with a worried expression on his face, wading knee-deep in the surf, and he had got Only by the scruff of the neck and pulled him along until there was solidity and he could stand. Only stumbled forward a few steps until he was completely free of the water, then wobbled for a moment and collapsed, panting and looking up at the figure who was kneeling beside him, stroking his head, saying soothing things to him.

After a while Only managed to rise unsteadily. The man coaxed him along, and they walked slowly for what must have been a mile or more to a small house behind a sand dune. The man opened the door and waited for Only to go inside. Immediately Only smelled the aromas of breakfast: bacon, eggs, toast, the old familiar things.

"Mary," the man called out in a cheerful voice, "we have a guest for breakfast."

"A guest?" came a startled call from the direction

in which the aromas emanated. "Why, Thomas, whatever do you mean?"

Back at the house in Wimbeldon there was no Sunday morning breakfast. George and Alice had made their way back to port in the dark, their sorrow hanging over the *Silkie* like a pall of New England fog. With as few words as necessary they had secured the little boat and walked to Burt's cabin and told him the grim news. His head hung as low as theirs.

The drive home was the same. Only the green glare of the dashboard lights; no radio, no music. Occasionally Alice would sob, and in his own way George tried to fight back tears.

"He was such a good dog," she said finally. "He was so kind."

"I was pretty hard on him with that leash business," George conceded. "I know I must have jerked him around too much."

"I don't know what to do . . . I just don't," Alice said.

"There isn't anything much," George said softly, shaking his head. "I guess we could come back down tomorrow and go out and . . . take a look or something."

"I can't bear him being out there, all alone, I mean, with the fish and the . . ." She let the sentence fade away.

"I know it's no consolation," he said, "but drowning is supposed to be the easiest way. . . . I mean, there's not supposed to be pain or anything, like if he had been hit by a car. . . ."

"We need to do *something*. We can't just let it go at this," she said bitterly.

"Like I said, we can come back in the morning and . . ."

"I know," she said quietly. "I'll get some flowers. There're still a few left in the garden that he didn't dig up. And we can get some dirt, fill up his bowl with it and"—she began to sob again— "and go back out and drop the flowers in the water, and the dirt from his garden, so he won't just be . . . alone."

"Sure, babe, we'll do it first thing," George said.

"Where do you suppose he came from?" asked the lady with iron-gray hair.

"Like I said," the older man replied, "I was just walking down the beach, and he was out there in the ocean. I thought I heard a bark, then didn't see anything, then I saw him get caught up in the surf and thrown around and I fished him out half-drowned. I don't know anybody 'round here's got any kind of dog looks like that. Too bad he doesn't have on a collar with an owner's name. Could be a stray—or he maybe even fell off a boat."

"Fell off a boat?" the woman said.

"Can happen," the man said. "You know, maybe I'll phone around to a couple of boatyards, and give a call to the marine police. Maybe somebody reported him."

Alice had found some orange lily blossoms and some white begonias and nasturtiums and was arranging them absently in her hand when George appeared in the doorway. Alice looked up at him tearfully, but with a wistful smile, and she gently rubbed her stomach. "I wish he . . . or she . . . whatever it's going to be, could have known him," she said.

George nodded ruefully. "Anything I can do?"

"His bowl's over there." She pointed to a large red plastic container. "You can fill it up with some dirt. Maybe from one of his holes," she said. George obeyed silently and cursed the luck and himself as well.

"It's such a beautiful day," Alice said. "Not a cloud in the sky."

Somewhere in the distance a church bell rang.

Burt had been up for a while and was working at some task in the boatyard when he heard the phone ring. He wiped his hands as he went into the office and answered it. He did not recognize the voice on the other end or understand the question that was being asked.

"Do you know anyone who lost a dog?" the caller said. It was an even, dignified tone of voice. Burt frowned.

"Dog?" he said. "This is a boatyard, mister, we don't have no pound here."

"No, what I mean," the caller said, "is, well, this sounds a little far-fetched I know, but I was walking on the beach this morning and fished a great big dog out of the ocean and thought possibly he might have fallen off . . ."

"Good grief. What kind of dog?" Burt shouted when it registered on him. "A great big furry dog?"

"Yeah, that's him I guess. I forget what kind you call them. Got no tail."

"You found that dog! You found Only? He's okay?"

"Bit waterlogged I'd say, but he's already eaten most of my breakfast."

"Where, in God's name?"

"Well, we're down here about five miles west of Hyannis. Right on the beach."

"You don't know it, mister, but you're sure gonna make a couple of people happy. That dog fell overboard yesterday afternoon about nine miles offshore. The owners looked for hours and give him up as lost. I hardly ever seen such sad people. I don't believe it! What's your number? Wait till I call them and tell them."

"Where are they now?" the man asked.

"Back up in the city. Went back last night. How can I tell them to locate you?"

"Well, I'll tell you what," the man said. "My wife and I have to go back ourselves today. Early. We're leaving in a couple of hours. I think it might be easier if I drop him off at your yard, if that's okay."

"Well, sure it is," Burt said. "Or I can come get him myself."

"No, no," the man said. "No bother. You're on our way. We kind of like him. Sweet dog. Can't believe he was out in the water all that time—that'd be almost twelve hours or more."

Burt shook his head. "I can't believe it either."

George and Alice pulled away from the curb and were gone just before the phone began ringing with Burt's happy news waiting at the other end of the line. In the back seat they had the flowers and the dog bowl and Only's collar, a few old bleached-out steak bones George had found while he was digging for the dirt to put in the bowl and also a ratty tennis ball Only liked to play with. They left the terrible leash behind. The ride back down to the shore was not much better than the ride back the night before, but they were trying to be cheerful.

"He wouldn't have wanted us to be unhappy," Alice said. "Remember how when we fought he'd go upstairs or scratch to get out to his garden, and then he'd come around to one of us?"

"Yeah," George said, "I remember."

Burt had made a quick trip to a little country store when George and Alice arrived, and when he returned he didn't notice their car in the yard or see them sitting forlornly in the cockpit of the *Silkie*. He did, however, see another car pull up with an elderly man driving it and Only's enormous shaggy face peering out the rear window. Only was beside himself as soon as he realized he was in the boatyard and saw Burt, and then he knew everything was going to be all right. He dashed out of the car and bounded around in the office while Burt explained to the man he had not been able to reach the Martins by phone. They talked for a few moments more about how Only came to be lost and saved, and as they talked, Only wandered out into the yard and ran down toward the *Silkie*.

But just as he reached the beginning of the wooden pier he hesitated. He could see George and Alice sitting in the cockpit, facing each other, talking softly. He took a few tentative steps toward them, then sat down uncertainly on his haunches, for it suddenly occurred to him that perhaps they were angry with him, that maybe he had done something wrong.

"I brought two bottles of wine," Alice said, "one for us, and one—well, I thought we might open it . . . pour it into the . . ."

George looked at the label. It was a Lafite '57, one he had been saving for some special occasion. Momentarily he felt an urge to object, to suggest perhaps that they use the other bottle, but in that same instant he damned well realized this wasn't the time to say anything about something like that, so he just nodded, then started to get up and take the cover off the tiller but suddenly froze in midrise. He looked in astonishment for a few moments at the big black nose and long pink tongue protruding from the mass of fur that was seated at the opposite end of the pier, watching them.

"Alice," George said calmly and slowly, as though he were speaking to a child, "I don't want you to say anything for a second, but I want you to look at what I think I see."

Seven

~~~

For a long while after his miraculous salvation, Only became the center of attention in the Martin household. So great was their joy that even George wept happily as they hugged and cuddled him, and he bounced and pawed in relief that they weren't angry. George and Alice bestowed their profuse gratitude on the white-haired old man who had pulled Only from the ocean and George several times attempted to offer a reward to him, pulling out a twenty-dollar bill from his wallet. It was only after he refused the third time that Burt was able to get George aside long enough to whisper in his ear that, despite his dress, the elderly man was not a beach-comber but, in fact, as Burt had learned from his earlier conversation, the chief judge of a circuit court of appeals.

"Greatgodamighty," George mumbled in aston-ishment and rolled his eyes to the ceiling.

When they got home that afternoon, Alice cooked

a big pot roast, and Only got the lion's share. Thereafter, his daily walks seemed to be longer, and he was let free more in the little park.

On one of these occasions he had an encounter that stirred strange feelings within him.

It was late summer and a cool evening, and Only was browsing contentedly among some shrubs when suddenly he saw a nose and a big pair of eyes peering at him from the opposite side of a bush. Only stuck his face into the bush and found himself staring directly at the happy and, to him, appealing visage of another dog the likes of which he had not seen before. She—it *was* a she—was large, nearly Only's size, but with much shorter fur, a beautiful reddish brown, and a long, evenly pointed snout, big gray eyes and floppy ears.

Only withdrew himself from the shrub and rushed around to the other side. The other dog (Blossom was her name, he was to learn later) stood by coyly as Only performed the requisite sniffing and smelling procedure, and then the two of them romped together for a while, nipping and nuzzling and galloping around the open grassy park. Only had of course done this kind of thing before with other dogs, but there was something different about that afternoon, a kind of magical summer's day, clear and brisk, with almost a hint of autumn in the air. But it was Blossom that caused the most profound difference on that day, for Only began to feel a rush of unexplainable desire that tingled his entire body and caused him to strut and prance and behave in a way that mystified even him.

"Looks like we've got a friendship going here," George said to the man to whom Blossom belonged. The two of them were standing under a large maple tree, each holding a leash.

"What kind of dog is that?" George asked.

"She's just a mutt," the man answered. "Name's Blossom. We found her at the dog pound about a year or so ago. I think they were going to put her to sleep, and my wife and I decided to go look for a dog for our kids. She turned out to have a real good disposition. Hard to say what she is though."

"Might be a bit of setter in her," George observed.

"Yep, that's what I thought too—and maybe something like spaniel, but I expect she's just a mix of a lot of things. All-American Dog, they say. Yours is a real beauty though. What's his name?"

"Only," George said casually. The man gave George a queer look, raised his eyebrows, then nodded and gazed back to where the two dogs were romping.

"How'd he get a name like Only?" the man finally asked.

"It's a long story," George said. The man nodded again.

George allowed Only to play in the park an extraordinarily long time that afternoon, and when he finally called him for the leash Only felt a panicky twinge that he might not see Blossom again. As

George led him off he continued to look back at Blossom, who was standing alone silhouetted against the sunset and watching him.

Later, at dusk, George and Alice sat in the garden at a little table they had set up amidst Only's excavations. Only was lying on his stomach in a corner, letting the bricks cool his stomach, his head resting between his paws, trying to understand this new and perplexing sensation he was experiencing.

"I think our Only's growing up," George said casually.

"How so?" Alice asked. She was leaning back, her stomach huge under a flowing ankle-length dress.

"He seems to have found a girlfriend."

"Oh, how wonderful!" Alice cried.

"Well, not really," George said. "I mean, I don't know what's going on in his mind, but there was this other dog today at the park, and he was really showing his stuff for her."

"A little girl dog," Alice said sweetly, looking over happily at Only, who had lifted his eyelids slyly in acknowledgment.

"This one's just a mutt, unfortunately," George said.

"So what?" Alice retorted in surprise.

" 'So what' is that he's not going to breed with a mutt," George said firmly.

"Why not?" Alice demanded.

"What do you mean, 'why not'?" George replied. "Here we are with a purebred dog that cost us hundreds of dollars, and you'd have him mated with a mongrel?"

"Well, if he likes her . . ."

"Likes her!" said George. "What the devil does that have to do with it, Alice? He's a dog. He's getting to the age where pretty soon he'll be onto any female he can lay his paws on. It doesn't matter to a dog what he, ah . . . goes after as long as it's in heat."

"I'll bet it does," Alice said knowingly.

"Look Alice, when the time comes we're going to find a female sheepdog of the best stock we can and mate them and maybe be able to turn a buck out of this animal. He's already eating us out of house and home."

"George!" Alice said, "how can you say that?"

"Okay, okay," he waved her off. "But you know what I mean. If we breed him, it just makes good sense to breed him properly."

Alice grumbled something about George being hardhearted and she returned to some knitting she was doing. From his corner of the garden, Only stared at them both from beneath furrowed brows.

Autumn galed its way into Wimbeldon, the days grew shorter again, and the leaves dropped off the trees and covered Only's garden where he sat day after day, occupying himself by occasionally digging another hole or waiting patiently for the cat to make some error in judgment and give him a chance to get

at it. This did not occur, though he came pretty close
several times. He did not see much of Blossom
either—perhaps four or five times in as many
weeks—but whenever he did his heart raced anxiously, and the two of them dashed side by side
through the park, sometimes getting tangled and
winding up in a scrambling heap on the ground.
When it came time to go, Only sometimes became
obstinate and had to be tugged away by George. The
snows came and with it the bitter cold, and then one
night George and Alice drove away hurriedly and
did not come back that night nor the next morning,
and then George returned alone. He fed Only and
took him for a short walk, then showered and left
again, returning late at night. This went on for
several days, through Sunday, Only realized, because
there was no pot roast, and he was beginning to get
concerned, except that George seemed happy
enough. Only sensed that if anything were wrong,
George would have shown it.

Then one morning the following week, Alice returned. George was with her, but she also had in her
arms a small squealing bundle. She knelt down with
it and gently summoned the curious Only to have a
look. What he saw mystified him. It was the tiniest
human he had ever seen, red-faced, with minute
little hands and fingers and almost bald-headed and
it looked at him in wide-eyed astonishment. He
noticed it had the same eyes as Alice, bright violet.
Only approached tentatively, somehow knowing

that this new arrival was of special import and that he should be cautious and reserved in his investigation. He nosed up to the bundle and stood looking at the creature inside it for a moment. He gazed up at George, who was smiling, then at Alice who was beaming and talking soothingly to Only.

"Only," she said, "this is Caroline." She also introduced Caroline to Only, using the same kind of baby talk he remembered from his own puppyhood. He inched closer and craned his neck forward. The baby's eyes got larger, and suddenly she reached out with one of her tiny hands and grabbed his big black nose. Only froze while the diminutive fingers twisted around the nose. Then he shot out his long pink tongue and lapped it around the baby's hand and arm like the trunk of an elephant. The infant recoiled with a shriek and Only, not knowing what else to do, did the first instinctive thing that came to him—he lapped out again with his tongue to lick the baby's face. At this, Alice swept the bundle out of his reach and barked, "No!" George, standing behind her, made some kind of move toward Only, and he realized he must have done the wrong thing and shrank back in fear and embarrassment, wishing he had a tail like other dogs so he could put it between his legs. This was going to be more complicated than he'd thought.

Days piled upon days, weeks upon weeks and months upon months, and George and Alice's attention continued to be concentrated on little Caroline.

Only got his share, of course, but it was decidedly smaller, and there were times when he felt shunted aside completely. He would sit for hours in his garden, even in bitter cold, and his contemplations became more profound.

Several things disturbed him. One was his own idea of who, or at least what, he was. He knew he was not like Alice or George or even little Caroline, who was so small and helpless; he also knew that he felt things that George and Alice did not know he felt. He had urges that came upon him like waves. Sometimes he desperately felt a need to run free, to be able to do what they could and he could not— just to open the door and walk outside and go where he wanted. These wishes tugged at him: to do, to see, to experience. Other, darker and less fathomable impulses seized him, too, from time to time. What he did not know was that for generation upon generation his breed had been used to herd, and it did not herd by nipping and barking as the newer, smaller, terrier-type sheepdogs did. Old English sheepdogs were bred large and powerful and they moved sheep about simply by manhandling (or doghandling) them, shouldering and bumping the herd along; physically overpowering a wayward sheep back into the flock. Although his breed had not been used for this duty in many years, it was somehow buried far, far down in his brain. When the new spring arrived with its warmth and longer days and then summer again, George would take

Only and little Caroline to the park, and there were times when his herding instinct overpowered him. If he saw Caroline toddling like a stray he would gently shoulder her back toward George. But these efforts were almost automatically met with a reproach, and Only had to wrestle violently within himself to resist them. Back in his garden sometimes he would brood. There seemed nothing he could do, no deed he could perform to make himself feel useful, no single thing that was his domain and his alone, except the garden that he resolved to guard against dangerous encroachment. Sorrowfully the only encroachment was tendered by the cat, and he seemed powerless even to deal with it.

It did not come to him as a flash of an idea, nor was it something he had dwelled on constantly, but over the weeks and months, on into another autumn and even another winter, a gloomy and harshly unsettling feeling began to take hold of Only. He began to feel worthless.

Eight

～～～

THAT NEXT YEAR ALICE HAD ANOTHER BABY, ALSO A girl, which they named Kimberly. But while she was devoting her time to the care of the children, Alice was also undergoing a somewhat radical change in her own life. The unsettled mood of the country had filtered down into Wimbeldon, and Alice began to embrace a variety of ideals and political causes that were against the grain of her upbringing and George's as well. While he remained fairly fixed in his thoughts, Alice became more and more involved with what was called the New Left.

At first her approach to it was purely from a humanitarian, idealistic standpoint. She truly hated the idea of war, and war was raging in Asia with death tolls mounting weekly. Slowly her attachment became more overt, and she began participating in marches and demonstrations and found a new set of friends who taught her everything from how to smoke dope to assembling a Molotov cocktail. She let her hair grow out long and frizzy and adopted a new style of dress, abandoning plaid skirts and blouses and jackets for ratty blue jeans she bought from a surplus store and T-shirts with slogans on them, or formless ankle-length cotton dresses. She put away her high-heeled shoes for sandals or sneakers or went barefoot. Also she stopped wearing jewelry and underwear.

In the beginning George, whose philosophy and style of clothing remained unchanged, believed it was just a phase she was going through. When Alice would try to draw him into discussions about her feelings he avoided them, until, frustrated, she would instigate a fight by raising the sound of the argument. Shouting ensued. In time, George began to be annoyed and anxious over their future because he began to realize that Alice was changing from the person he had married into a strong-willed, independent woman going in the opposite direction from himself and from the way he believed the family should be raised.

As the disharmony between George and Alice grew, there was also an increasing amount of chaos in the household because of the small children, and Only, having been removed as the center of attention when little Caroline came along, was even further removed with the arrival of Kimberly and with Alice's preoccupation with her various political-action groups. As he tried to adjust to this changing status he became anxious and sometimes

brooding and, with ever-increasing frequency, retreated to the sanctity of his garden.

Not that things were all that bad. There was still
pot roast on Sunday, and he still got his walks in the
afternoon and at night he sat inside with George and
Alice and the children, and they would play with
him and sometimes ride on his back, and little
Kimberly, when she was old enough to walk, would
sometimes toddle over and tweak his nose or pull on
one of his ears, but he endured it all stoically,
wanting to serve at least some kind of purpose, even
if it was nothing more than being a toy or plaything
for the girls.

The single thing he missed most was Blossom.
Something had gone awry, some change in schedule,
he did not know what, but each time he was taken to
the park, Only immediately scanned the area, his
heart beating in anticipation, but she was not to be
found. Once he saw her just as he had been put on
the leash to be led home. Her owner had arrived on
the far side of the park, beneath a group of trees, and
was removing Blossom's leash when Only spotted
her. He stopped dead still and dug his claws into the
ground and began to pull George toward her.
George, not knowing, or not appreciating, wrestled
him around with a jerk and dragged him to the
street, coughing and sputtering as the collar choked
him. Just as he lost sight of her, Only let out one of
his rare, deep "woofs" and as he was led across the

street he heard a faint bark in the distance. It was an afternoon in March, neither winter nor yet spring, and all the way home Only's head hung low. That night he barely touched his dog food and lay sullenly in a corner of the living room while George and Alice sat on opposite sides of the room, with the two girls playing on the floor between them. George was reading a newspaper, and Alice was studying some kind of literature that inspired her to occasionally say out loud, "Oh wow," or "Really!"

"I think," George said, "it's about time for Only to perform his biological function."

Alice looked up quizzically. "You mean he needs to go out?" she asked.

"No," said George, "I think he needs to be bred."

"To whom?" Alice asked.

"To what," George responded evenly. "I think you should get in touch with Dr. Peltz tomorrow and have him look into locating a dog of good stock we can put Only with."

"What brought this on?" Alice asked suspiciously.

"Oh, I don't know. Hard to believe, but he'll be six years old this spring. Today when I took him for his walk, that other dog, the mutt, was at the park just as I was leaving. I think he saw her, and he balked at coming home."

"Well, why didn't you let him stay for a minute?" Alice asked.

"For heaven's sake, Alice," George said. "He'd

been there half an hour. I wanted to get home. It was cold."

"But if he really wanted to see her you might have."

"Doggone it, Alice!" George said, his voice raised a pitch or two. "If he's going to be bred, it's going to be done the right way; so will you please call Dr. Peltz in the morning and get him on the case?"

"You really don't understand things, do you?" Alice said exasperatedly.

"Better than you might think," George retorted. The silence that followed sent an electric tension through the room. The kids became quieter, and Only got up and walked to the door to the garden and pawed it so they would let him outside.

It wasn't long after that, perhaps a week or so by Only's reckoning, that he was loaded into the family car, a new station wagon, and driven by Alice and George to the office of Dr. Peltz. Immediately he recoiled when he saw the little red brick building. All he knew from previous experience was that every time he went in there somebody would stick him with a needle or poke around at something that hurt already. He could never figure out why they did that. It seemed like some kind of punishment, but it rarely happened after he knew he had done something wrong. Humans were a strange sort, he thought darkly as he was led into the office by his leash.

Only relaxed a little when he saw Dobie. The old man's smile and soothing chatter made him feel better. Dobie took off the leash and slipped a rope around his neck but chucked him behind the ears and giggled and led him through the waiting room occupied by half-a-dozen people with a variety of sullen-looking animals at their sides or in their laps. There were three dogs, including a vicious-looking chow, and two cats and a woman with a child who sat with a caged hamster.

Dr. Peltz was waiting in the examining room, but this time Only wasn't lifted onto the hateful table. The vet gave him a quick going-over, looking into his eyes and pinching open his mouth and looking down his throat and then he tousled his hair and patted him on the top of his head.

"Well, let's hope it takes," the vet said. "What I've found is about the best that you can do outside of the Fezziwig line. She's a real beaut—big for her age and a bit darker on the saddle, but the litter ought to be perfect."

"Where . . . where is she?" Alice asked.

"We've got her out back," Dr. Peltz said. "She came in a while ago. Dobie picked her up at the airport, and she's still a little unsettled—they tranquilized her for the flight. She'll be okay later this afternoon. Came into heat about two days ago, that's when the owner called me. She'll be ready by tonight."

"How, I mean, where, do you do—do they—do *it?*" George asked curiously.

"Oh, we've got a place in the back. A little room, got straw on the floor and all. Dobie looks after them."

"You suppose we ought to provide a little candle-light and champagne?" George quipped.

"How will he know, ah, what to do?" Alice asked with a concerned look.

"He'll know," Peltz said darkly.

"Lord," George said, "when I was a kid, we . . . well, I'd heard you lock 'em up in a garage or something."

"It's about the same thing," Peltz said profession-ally. "But Dobie knows what to do—if there's any problem, he's got some equipment to sort of help things along." The veterinarian smiled, and Dobie, who was stroking Only's head, nodded knowingly.

"I'll take real good care of 'im, Miz Martin. Don't you worry none. I'll—"

"Why don't you go ahead and take him back there now," Peltz cut in. "The sooner the better."

Two days later the Martins received the expected call from Dr. Peltz.

"Well," the vet said, "I am embarrassed to say that nothing has happened."

"Nothing at *all?*" George asked increduously.

"I have never seen anything like it. He just sits

there on his haunches. Won't have anything to do with her."

"Maybe something's wrong with *her* then," George offered.

"Checked that. She's ready, willing and able. It's *him.*"

"What do you suppose it is?"

"Can't say. Maybe he just doesn't want to for some reason. Checked him out too. He's got the equipment, and it's in order."

"Doesn't want to?" George said in astonishment.

"Like I said," Peltz said curtly, "I've never seen anything like it before. All I can figure is, well, he's just obstinate."

"That he is," George said, "that he is." He put down the phone and walked into the kitchen where Alice was preparing supper.

"Guess what," he said sourly.

"I heard," she said.

"Can you beat that," George said. "Just sits there like the Great Gawd Bud and watches her. He *must* be retarded."

"He had a choice and he made it," Alice retorted.

"For heaven's sake," George cried, "he's a dog! He's supposed to behave like a dog."

"Has he ever?" Alice said. She was stirring something on the stove and did not look up.

"Rarely," George conceded. He walked over to the pot Alice was stirring.

"What's that?" he asked curiously.

"It's wheat grain and vegetables," she said. "I think this family should eat less meat. It's not good for you."

"You're turning us into vegetarians now?" George asked in astonishment.

"Well, I might become one. I've been thinking about it lately. But I'll still cook you meat, and a little for the girls. But in general, I don't think it's a good thing anymore."

"Greatgodamighty," George groaned. He peered again into the pot Alice was stirring.

"It looks like birdseed and mush," he hissed, and walked out of the room.

Alice picked up Only at the vet's office the following morning. Somehow he sensed that he had either done something he was not supposed to or *not* done something he was supposed to, but he felt a little funny on the ride home and he sat in the back of the station wagon looking out of the rear window. He couldn't for the life of him figure out why they had put him in that room with that awful other dog. She was nice-looking enough, but her attitude was, well, she *had an attitude.* When Dobie had let him in the room, it was as though she had been waiting there for him just like a spider. There was none of the coyness or subtlety Blossom exuded; this one just stared him in the eye as if to say, "Let's get on with it!"—whatever "it" was. Only really wasn't sure. He felt something, a disturbing urge that he *ought* to be doing something, but he hadn't been exactly certain how to proceed, and then Dobie came in and started . . . well, whatever was supposed to have been going on, Only hadn't wanted any part of it and he was darned happy to be out.

"A disaster," George said when he got home from work that night. Only had been lying in a corner, half-asleep, dreaming of open fields and flowers and tall grass, a place where he could run and run and run . . .

"A miserable failure," George continued. He was standing with his hands on his hips in the doorway, looking at Only. "We have raised this sanctimonious furball who does nothing but eat, sleep and lie around in the yard, and who, when given one chance to do something valuable, what does he do?"

Only cringed from these aspersions, drew himself in close, tucked his head between his paws and tried to make himself as small as possible.

"Oh, George," Alice said matter-of-factly, "it isn't the end of the world."

"Do you realize that now *we* are going to have to pay for that dog to get shipped back all the way to Philadelphia. It's going to cost more than a hundred dollars."

"I told you he wanted that other one, what's her name? Blossom?"

George threw up his hands in exasperation. "Nobody listens to what I say! All day long I sit behind a desk and listen to other people's financial problems. All day long I have at my disposal hundreds of thousands of dollars of other people's money that I can't touch a cent of. I come home at night half the time to find you dressed up in some kind of Halloween costume on your way out to a political cabal discussing the overthrow of the very institution that pays our bills. Our two small children are growing up as Marxists, and that big oaf over there in the corner refused to have even the courtesy to do what comes completely natural to him!"

"George," Alice said calmly, "why don't you make yourself a drink and settle down. You're beginning to rave."

"Rave, hell," George said, "I'm beginning to lose my mind."

"You'll get over it," Alice said cheerfully.

Only got up and padded over to the garden door and whimpered to go outside.

George's speech that night, his frustration, his dissatisfaction with the roll life's dice were taking for him was fairly typical of the mood in the Martin home. There was discord and trouble and resentment, and with each day and week and month it seemed to get worse. Beyond being powerless to intervene, to make some small conciliatory contribution as he had when it was just the three of them, Only now began to see himself as somehow part of the problem.

Then one day, a Sunday the following winter, after a particularly difficult week of arguments, tension and bitterness, something very unsettling happened. George began packing things in boxes and suitcases and bags. The girls had been sent off to play with friends. Alice was helping George with his things and neither of them talked much. The tension seemed to be gone, replaced by an air of sadness and relief.

"Would you like to take the coffee pot?" Alice asked quietly.

"No, it's okay, I'll get another one," he said.

"Oh, go ahead and take it. I can use instant. I don't even drink coffee much anyway."

"It's okay," George said.

Later in the afternoon, when everything had been packed and loaded, George went out to the garden where Only was lying in a little patch of sunlight. George stood in the doorway, and Only got up and came over to him, and George sat down on the steps and took Only's big head in his lap.

"Well, feller," he said, "I guess you don't understand any of this, do you?" It sounded almost as if he expected an answer. Only licked George's hands and nuzzled in closer.

"I'll be back to see you," he said, "and we can take our walks, sometimes. And you can come and visit me with the girls, all right?" Only put a paw on George's knee and tried to crawl up in his lap, but George cuddled his head and touseled his ears and stood up. Alice was standing behind them in the doorway, tears beginning to brim in her eyes.

"All right," George said, "I guess that's it." He turned, and when he saw Alice the two of them stood looking at each other for a moment, then George walked to her and put his arm around her waist and she put hers around his and they shut the door. Only moved around to the window where he could see them walking until they reached the front door. George gave Alice a hug and then was gone.

Alice let Only inside and went into the kitchen and puttered for a little while, then she suddenly threw down a dishrag and marched into the room where the liquor cabinet was and poured a large tumbler of whiskey and took it up to the bedroom. Only could hear her sobbing softly. After a few minutes he followed her up there and sat by her bed for a long time.

With George gone, things were different. He came back on weekends and picked up the girls and Only, too, sometimes, and they went to an apartment George had found on the other side of town. It was a newer apartment and there was a swimming pool and a little lawn, but Only wasn't allowed to play on the lawn or by the pool. They would go for walks in his new neighborhood, but Only didn't much like it here.

Back home, Only felt more and more alone. Alice seemed nervous and edgy and not very happy and she flustered easily at small things. Only tried to stay by her as much as he could but succeeded mainly in getting in her way, and she snapped at him and at the girls too. He had a lot of time on his paws also, because Alice had taken a job in a little gift shop and was gone most of the day while the girls were at school, and Only found himself getting on edge too.

Relegated to the garden, his sole companion was the cat on the wall or an occasional squirrel or bird. His afternoon walks seemed to be shorter, because Alice couldn't leave the girls for long and had to fix supper. Sometimes different men would come at night and take Alice out, but she would always come home later.

One glum and misty day in autumn just before dusk, Alice took him to the park and there on the far side beneath a set of children's swings was Blossom. Freed from his leash, Only rushed toward her, and when she saw him coming she turned toward him, but as he closed she squatted down, her long tail between her legs. Only had been running so fast he skidded when he tried to stop and began to sniff and bounce up and down around her. Blossom seemed somehow changed. All of a sudden, Only got the strangest feeling of his life: something about Blossom, some smell, some seductive aroma. Without warning, an impulse, dark and unexplained, seized him, and he pounced upon her back in a rush of heat and fervor. Just as quickly, he felt himself being dragged off by strong hands. It was the man who brought her to the park.

"No!" he said sternly. "Get away!" He menaced Only with an upraised hand. Only, startled, looked up at him with hurt and surprise in his eyes.

"Go on—get away!" the man growled.

Alice had walked up with a concerned look on her face.

"I'm sorry," the man said, "but Blossom's—well, I don't think we need any puppies right now, if you know what I mean. . . ."

"Only," Alice said tenderly but firmly, "come here!" Only looked up at her with pleading in his eyes.

"Come on," Alice said. She was holding the leash, slapping it in the palm of her hand.

"I'm sorry," the man said again.

"I understand," Alice said. Blossom was sitting on her haunches looked at Only with large watery eyes, her tongue hanging out. Only looked at Alice, then back at Blossom, and then at the man, who had stepped over to Blossom and put her leash on. Alice snapped on Only's leash as he watched Blossom being led away.

"We've got to go home now," Alice said soothingly. I know how you feel. But that's the way life is sometimes," she said. For an instant Only stood his ground, refusing to budge, but Alice gave him a firm tug, and he got to his feet and toddled reluctantly behind her, all the while looking back at Blossom, who was being led off in the opposite direction. They reached the top of the hill, and there, Only balked. He sat down on his haunches and dug his claws into the grass as he watched Blossom fading into the misty evening. Suddenly he did something he had never done before; instinct as on other occasions, simply overcame him. This time, out of some inner pain and rage and want, Only threw back his head and began to howl pitifully and loudly.

He howled two or three times, then felt Alice's arms around his neck, holding him closely. He stopped howling and looked at her and saw her eyes were filled with tears.

All that night and the next day and the next, Only brooded. It had been a rainy week with leaves blowing and dark, ominous storm clouds sailing overhead, but still he preferred to be outside, in his garden. He curled up under the eaves and let the rain drop down in front of him and found himself pondering his destiny. The same day the storm ended, Only had clearly reached a crossroads.

He was torn between two masters, Alice and the girls and George, whom he also missed—and his own urges. Every fiber of his instinct told him he had been put into the world to work, to be useful, to herd something or whatever. But on the other hand he had been raised as almost human, and so he also felt a yearning to do as humans could do, to see, to experience somehow things for himself, to control his destiny. Yet here he was, shunted into the garden the way a crazy old relative might be relegated to an attic room. The years of his life flashed by him in an unsatisfied montage, and also, there was Blossom.

It was a Sunday, this bright afternoon after the storm, and the sky turned that clear cloudless blue, and the New England light fell in soft patterns on the golds and burnished-red leaves and still bright green shrubbery. There had been no pot roast today, as there had not been since the day George left, for Alice had come down hard against the consumption of meat. The sun had fallen behind the brick wall, the cat had retired to its own environs, and the girls were upstairs in their playroom.

Alice was in the den with a fire in the fireplace, reading something, when Only scratched to get inside. She got up absently and let him in, still reading as she walked back to her chair and sat down. Only looked up the stairs, considered going up and poking his head in on Caroline and little Kimberly, then decided against it. He meandered over to Alice and rested his head on the arm of the chair and began to lick her hand. Without taking her eyes off her reading, Alice patted him on the head and scratched him behind the ears. He lapped out with his tongue at her fingers, feeling a rush of great unknowable sadness mingled with an odd sensation of anticipation and wonder.

Only backed away and went down the little hallway toward the front door. He passed his leash and collar hanging on the coathook, stopped for a moment to drink some water out of the toilet, and then, at the door, he stealthily lifted his left paw and wedged a nail in the tiny crevice between the jamb and the door. It was not tightly shut. He pulled, and the door moved inward slightly. He pulled again, and it moved once more.

Then he wedged his nose in the little opening and nudged the door open and when his head was firmly set he shouldered the door wide and stuck his head outside.

All was quiet on the little street. Not a soul moved. Lights were on in most of the houses. He took a few more tentative steps until he was halfway down the quaint old brick sidewalk and stood there for a few moments, looking in either direction, then trotted off to the end of the block in the direction of the park. At the corner he paused again and took a long, backward look at the house. He knew what he was doing was wrong, but it was too late to worry about that now. He turned his face to the quiet streets and crossed to the opposite side and headed away in the fading light.

Nine

THE FIRST PLACE ONLY WENT WAS TO HIS PARK. IT WAS deserted except for two children playing basketball at the far end. There was no Blossom or for that matter any other dog. He nosed around for a while, feeling weird and a little nervous, then loped toward the trees across the baseball diamond and slouched among them furtively, suddenly stricken by the fear that at any moment he would hear Alice's stern voice apprehending him. He considered going back to the house. She might not have even noticed he was gone. But then a surge of courage engulfed him, and he strode out of the park, across the street, in the same direction which Blossom was usually taken away.

Once or twice he thought he caught her scent, but the days of rain since their last meeting had either obscured it or he was mistaken in the first place. He wandered down sidewalks past neat townhouses. The long shadows of evening had disappeared, and nightfall was complete. Only had traveled a considerable distance by now, crossing many blocks, including a main thoroughfare on which there was moving traffic. He noticed that the houses had begun to look different, their lawns were larger and they were set more widely apart. He turned down one street to find that it led nowhere and so he walked up on a lawn in between two houses and crossed a little wooded area and came out on another lawn and then on another street. It was all risky, exciting and new. He had lost track of time except that it must have been some hours now since he had nosed out of the door. He stopped to lap water from a puddle and continued on, not really knowing what direction he was taking. He decided that now it really didn't matter, that he was not going to find Blossom. There were just too many places, and he had gone a long, long way.

He came to a wide, quiet street, well lighted, and on the opposite side was another park, larger and more wooded than his own. He crossed and nosed around for a while, sniffing at the strange new smells of other dogs. There was a wire trash basket, filled nearly to the top, emitting the faint odor of food, and Only suddenly felt a pang of hunger. He poked around it for a while but couldn't get at anything, so he raised his paw and pushed it over. The garbage spilled out on the ground, and he began to root in it until he found the source of the smell—a half-eaten hot dog, which he gobbled up. He wandered a little farther and came upon a park bench. He lay down under it, the autumn breeze cool and eerie, and rested there for a while, intermittently drifting off to sleep, then waking fitfully. The night passed slowly. It was his first night absolutely alone since the time he'd spent floundering in the ocean, and somehow he felt unprotected, vulnerable to whatever might be against him. Once, when he awoke and looked around, he noticed a faint light, and then the sun began to brighten around him. He felt thirsty, and it took him a while to find a ditch where there was some bitter-tasting standing water. He drank his fill, then trotted off through the park, emerging in an entirely different neighborhood, with strange smells and a menacing air about it. The streets were unclean, but for Only this turned out to be a blessing, because there was food for him to pick at in the garbage. He passed narrow rows of houses, some of them with people sitting on the steps. Twice he approached some of these people, ambling up as he might during a walk in his own neighborhood, expecting to be petted or greeted fondly. Instead, he received gruff admonishments and was shooed off down the street. This neighborhood was huge, so ponderous, Only was amazed. He seemed to have walked for miles, but every street appeared the same. A few people paid him attention. On one corner were some boys, and as he came up to them, one began looking at him strangely and said something to the others, and the first suddenly tried to grab him. Only darted out of reach and loped away. The boy ran after him for half a block, but Only ran much faster, and the boy gave up. It scared him a little, somebody trying to grab him that way, but he knew he could outrun a human, so he wasn't much bothered by it. And then, just as he was feeling a little more secure in that thought, trouble struck when he least expected it.

He might have sensed it first and then heard it, but something caused him to turn his head around just as he had trotted past a dark alleyway. There was no warning, not a sound, a bark or a growl, just as it had been so many years before with the poodle—but there was a sudden rush of dog claws on the concrete sidewalk, and as he turned a large black thick-headed dog, its jaws open and fangs bared, sprang out of the alleyway charging and was upon him before he could turn to defend himself. The big dog pounced on Only's hindquarters, and Only felt himself giving way, bowled over and hitting the hard sidewalk and the pain as the other dog, now snarling, slashed deeply into his hip. Only tumbled over in a roll and stuck out his forepaws, trying to fend off the attacker and at the same time to regain his footing. He knew he should not let himself be turned onto his back. The big dog lunged for Only's throat just as Only had sprung back to his feet. Only dodged the snapping jaws and backed away and faced the other dog.

There wasn't time to think, to plan, to do anything

really, except defend himself; this much he knew. He had been in a few minor scrapes before, beginning with the nosebite by the poodle, and every so often in the park at home another dog had exhibited hostility, and two or three times he had gotten into a brief scuffle with a few bites being administered here and there, but invariably it was broken up by George or Alice or the owner of the other dog before things got out of hand.

This was very different. Not only were George and Alice not there to intervene, but he could now tell very plainly that this dog, whatever his reasons, was not merely posturing or trying to demonstrate his authority. There was a wild gleam in the yellowish eyes of this brute that bespoke pure savagery. For the first time in his life, Only was frightened to the point of panic. This other dog meant to kill him.

They stood there for that instant after Only had regained his feet, glaring at each other, and the other dog began to move slowly in a crouch to Only's left side. Only wanted to run, but he sensed that the other dog could probably catch him and throttle him from behind. He had no choice but to try to stand his ground here. In a split-second's time he noticed the big dog's paws tense, and then it was upon him in a leap, tearing at the back of his neck and growling wildly. It was fortunate that Only's fur was so thick, otherwise he might have been a goner, but all the other dog came up with was a mouthful of fur, and it gave Only time to duck down and snap out at the black dog's leg, just above the paw. Only crunched and twisted his neck, pulling the other dog on top of him. He hung on for all he had, and they tumbled into the street. The black dog had spat out the fur and slashed at Only's floppy ear. Only felt it tear near the end, and a current of pain caused him to yelp a stifled cry, still holding on to the leg. Only tried to improve his grip, but that was a mistake because the other dog jerked free and slashed out at Only's head, raking him on the snout and leaving a long ugly gash.

Then in all his pain and fear something overtook Only, a sensation not of courage, but of recklessness, of complete abandon and unbridled animal savagery. For the next moments he had no feelings other than survival and hatred. Fangs lashed out and tore at flesh and fur; howls of rage filled the air—everything became a red-hazed blur as the two dogs crashed against each other on the hard concrete of the street and sidewalk. After an interminable nightmare of time, the other dog stopped pressing his attack though he stood growling in heaving pants, his tongue hanging out of his mouth. Only, panting heavily as well, watched him for a moment, then began slowly backing up, waiting warily for the next lunge. But the other dog did not make a move. He stood there and growled, and Only stood his ground for a moment or two, neck bent down, gasping for breath. Then he raised his head. Still the black dog did not move, so Only turned slowly away from him and began walking down the street. He purposely did not look back, but it was not from fear; rather it was a kind of disdain. He had not exactly won, but he certainly had not lost either, and he knew it.

Only walked stiff and aching for miles in this grim new part of town. Several times he was nearly struck by cars that whizzed chaotically by; there was much horn blowing; there were places where steam came up out of the streets and there was nothing but concrete and brick and steel. Only hurt badly from his wounds. The bite on his hip was deep, and his snout also stung badly—but the ear was worse. It was torn apart about an inch and a half, and the blood had dripped onto his fur and matted it. Every so often he would stop to drink from a stagnant puddle in an alleyway and lick at the cut on his lip, but he couldn't get at the cut on the ear. When it became too painful, though, he would bat it with his paw. To make things worse it began to rain. First a drizzle, then a downpour, as the night closed in again. Only wandered aimlessly along many streets. People gave him a wide berth, and he must have looked a disturbing sight; matted with blood and rain-bedraggled and with a confused, haunted look in his eyes.

Finally he seemed to come to the outskirts of this unwholesome place. There were fields, some fenced by wire, littered with rusty metal objects, but at least there was some grass around. He spent the night huddled beside a ditch under an overpass. All night long his wounds and the speeding traffic that rattled and roared above kept him awake. He was hungry, lonely and afraid and wanted to be back home, but something kept him from just getting up and trying to make his way back. Even if he could have found his way—which at this point was questionable—he had committed himself, and once Only decided he was going to do something, he became as tenacious as a terrier at a rabbit hole.

Original thoughts and ideas came to him slowly, but once they took hold, they became implanted deeply and unshakably in his brain. Sometimes he wished he were as smart as humans, but he realized he wasn't (this was one of his more original revelations). But he had amazing determination, and one of the things he was determined about was to get a look at this world humans inhabited. Being a dog was all right, but he yearned for the freedom to do as he pleased, even though so far the experience had not been very pleasant. At first the idea, more or less, had been to try to find Blossom, and after that he had left the book open. But even having failed to locate her he felt he had come too far to go back now. Even with the problems of finding things to eat, being pounced upon by the big black dog, having to stay out in the rain, and the gnawing, growing angst at the world that seemed not to care about him one way or the other, he rejected the idea of crawling back home. It just went against his grain, and that was that.

Morning came cool and gray with menacing clouds in the sky, and Only painfully hoisted himself to his feet, stiff and aching from his cuts and bruises. He walked for several miles, and the noise and clamor of the city seemed to recede behind him. For a while he followed some railroad tracks, in which direction he did not know, but it was fairly easy going. He came upon a garbage dump and picked around for a while, eating anything that looked halfway appealing. He even found bones with meat on them and for a moment considered burying them; then he decided against it, for it came to him that he might not pass this way again.

By late afternoon the railroad tracks led him to the outskirts of another town, and to another garbage dump, inhabited by scavenging birds and rats. Once a rat scurried up to him while he was gnawing on some garbage, and he growled at it, and it scurried away.

Only shied away from towns. Humans seemed hostile toward him and so did most other dogs. Every so often the railroad tracks would cross a trestle and there he would spend the night beneath the tracks. For days the clouds did not break, and the north wind howled, and occasionally he would be pelted by a stinging rain. Finally the tracks led up to what seemed to be another large town. He could see tall buildings in the distance and hear the noise of traffic and machinery, and he decided it was time to strike out in a different direction. He veered off the tracks into a dense field that led to a line of trees and suddenly he found himself in a forest.

The forest was pleasant at first. The trees were tall, and the underbrush sparse, and there were trails made by humans, and Only trotted along them contentedly. He saw a few squirrels and once he flushed a rabbit. But as the day wore on there were fewer trails, and the forest seemed to become deeper and more sinister, and by nightfall the only trails were those made by other animals. There was plenty of water to drink in this forest, little brooks and streams seemed to pop up quite often, and once he had to wade across one of them and at another he had to wander a long distance upstream to find a shallow fording spot, because ever since the incident in the ocean, he had been less than comfortable in any body of water whose bottom he could not touch with his paws.

But the big problem there in the forest was food. There was nothing: no dumps, no litter or trash to pick from. Late in the day Only had come across the half-rotted carcass of some animal. He sniffed at it, but it was repulsive-smelling, and he continued on, and now, as darkness came on, he thought solemnly that perhaps he shouldn't have been so finicky.

It was scary in the forest at night. There were gnarled trees and undergrowth so thick a snake couldn't wriggle through it, and Only was forced in the directions the forest wanted him to go, not the ones he might have chosen for himself. Large briars tore at his fur, once he was painfully entangled in a huge bush for nearly half an hour before he managed to extricate himself. That night he curled up at the foot of a tree, tired and hungry, and again didn't sleep well because he wasn't sure what dangerous things might suddenly come at him from the dark.

Next morning he continued on but discovered that the terrain was becoming more rocky and steep, though not much clearer of undergrowth. He found himself climbing sometimes over large rocks, and he seemed to be going *up*, someplace. By afternoon the undergrowth had thinned, but the going was much harder, because the rocks hurt the pads of his feet. And then it began to sleet.

The sleet began in a windy gust from a low bank of ominous-looking clouds, and continued to fall all that afternoon and into the next night, stinging his nose and eyes as he climbed upward and onward. He finally reached a clearing where the big trees suddenly stopped and there was only hard rock and small scrubby underbrush. The wind howled piteously. Looking up, he saw that he was on the slope of a big mountain. Only had never seen a mountain before, but he knew enough to realize that this was the kind of unknown obstacle that might pose a lot of difficulty.

At least he was out of the forest and could see where he was going. Pangs of hunger washed over him, and he felt weakened, and also, he had had no water since early morning. The sleet had stopped, and Only was picking his way along a ridge of particularly sharp rocks, when there was a strange-sounding *ping* below him, followed immediately by a loud report from somewhere below. Only stopped and looked down. He saw a tiny human figure standing at the edge of the treeline, with a red-and-black-checkered jacket and a brown hat, holding a long thing that looked like a stick. As he watched curiously, he saw a little white puff of smoke come from the end of the stick, and there was another *ping* just below him again and a little to his front. He stood there watching as the human raised the stick again to his shoulder. Then a larger human emerged from the woods and grabbed the smaller figure by the shoulder and snatched the stick away from him. There was some sort of animated conversation between the two, with the larger human shaking his head and pointing up at Only and shaking his finger in the smaller human's face. Only's immediate instinct was to make his way down to them, because he felt they might show him the way out of this place and also they might give him some food. Humans had always given him his food. As he watched, the larger human, who was also carrying a stick, handed the smaller human's stick back to him, and they began climbing up toward Only. There was something unsettling about this. Torn between the urge to climb down and meet these two, or to run away from them, Only chose the latter. He scrambled upward among the rocks and boulders and after a long while paused, panting and sore. He looked back and did not see them again so he continued on at a more leisurely pace. But as night began to come over the mountainside again, he sought the shelter of the forest, making his way down a treacherously steep incline until he reached the edge of the trees, where he spent the night, hungrier and more frightened than ever.

In the morning the gray billowing skies had not abated, and a mixture of rain and sleet spattered the forest floor through the trees. It took most of the day for Only to get to where the ground was fairly level again, and once more he was back in the tangled underbrush, and the hunger came viciously upon him. It was just at twilight, and Only had been following an animal path for a long while when he came upon a small pool of still water in a little clearing. He went to the water's edge and found the ground mushy and overgrown with brown reeds. He lapped at the water, then raised his dripping chin and caught a glimpse of movement just ahead of him.

It was a fowl of some kind, drifting slowly from behind some of the reeds. He had seen fowl before on the ponds near the ocean, but they were white, and this bird was dark-feathered, with a green head and wings and a touch of red. It seemed oblivious to his presence.

Only stood frozen in the mush. He was so hungry he had a slight dizzy spell and had to sit down but kept his eyes riveted on the bird. It was facing away from him, occasionally ducking its head under the water and bobbing back up with some sort of grass in its bill.

A dark and strange instinct swept over Only. His heart began to pound and he began to salivate. He had never killed a living thing, but this rush of instinct enveloped him as strongly as the uncontrolled surges he had when he was about to go under in the ocean, and when he had seen Blossom in the park that final time, and during the fight with the big black city dog. All other things were blotted out, and his thoughts existed on a primitive and single-minded urging. He made a tentative step forward in the chill water and sank to his elbows, then paused. The fowl was still bobbing its head underwater, unaware of him. He took several more steps to the edge of the tall reeds so that he was hidden behind them. Stealthily he crept along, crouched, his eyes unblinking, focused on the spot at the end of the reeds where the fowl had been bobbing. He could see little ripples in the water, rings that spread gently outward in the dim light. Again, time became meaningless; it might have been minutes, or hours. He was up to his belly in the water and almost out of the reeds when the fowl suddenly came into view again, paddling closer to him but at such an angle that it couldn't see him.

It got within several feet before it noticed him. In that instant he sprang at it and in midlunge he could see the terror and panic in the fowl's eyes as it flapped its wings and tried to lift itself into the air. But Only batted it down with a big paw and seized it by the neck before it could escape. The bird squawked horribly for a moment, but Only gave a terrific toss of his head, heard a snap, and the fowl went limp in his mouth. He carried it to the shore and dropped it on the mud bank where it twitched briefly, then lay completely still. He nosed at its breast and found it warm and soft with down. He picked it up again in his mouth, gently, and carried it back into the woods and again let it fall and then sat down with it between his paws and watched it for a long time. He finally nosed it over onto its side and sank his teeth into its back. He hit feathers and bone, and the taste was unsatisfactory, so he spat out the feathers and took a webbed foot into his mouth and tore away at it. It was tough and sinewy but it was nourishment. He went at the other foot and then the head, crunching it between his jaws. He chewed on until he had disemboweled the fowl and licked at the warmth of its innards. He sat there all night tearing away at the flesh, bloody and good, piece by piece.

Dawn came, its pink and rosy glow announced by the squawking of birds high in the trees. Only was finished with the last of the fowl, his stomach filled and satisfied. Just a few feathers and bones remained. He walked to the edge of the pond and bent over to lap some water and saw in his reflection that the fur around his chin was bathed in blood. He peered at the reflection, then drank deeply of the sweet water and licked the blood and water from his fur and shook himself and journeyed out again, feeling somehow fierce and more self-sufficient. He was on his own. This much he knew.

Ten

∽∾∿

"I DON'T KNOW HOW IT HAPPENED," ALICE SAID INTO the telephone weakly. "He must have nosed open the door somehow. I looked all over and drove around for two or three hours and I thought he'd come back this morning for sure. But I haven't seen a sign."

"Have you called the pound?" George asked from the other end of the line.

"Well, not yet. I suppose I should. I keep thinking he'll turn up. What are we going to do?"

"Well," George said, "You call the pound. I can't leave the office just now, but at lunchtime I'll get away and drive around and see if I can find him."

"I'll bet that girl dog—what's her name—Blossom? I'll bet she has something to do with this."

"Maybe," George said, "maybe." After they hung up he went to the boss and asked if he could leave for the rest of the day. "It's an emergency," he said.

"Poor old fool," George muttered to himself as he

drove toward Wimbledon, "if he gets in traffic he won't stand a chance."

With his belly full of the duck, Only set out again through the woods. Little spots of early morning sunlight filtered through the trees and danced on the forest floor. It had become open and less dense beneath the trees. There was a kind of mossy ground, damp from the week of rain. At the far end of the pond Only came on a beaver dam and saw the beaver lugging a piece of log on top of it. The beaver saw him, too, and posed itself to jump into the water, but Only simply exchanged glances and went on his way.

Suddenly the forest gave way to a great field. As he stepped from the edge of the trees, the late autumn sun burst forth from behind a lone white cloud in a grand explosion of warmth and brilliance. The field was filled with wildflowers: goldenrods, daisies. And beyond it were more open spaces, small hills with green fields and pastures, and in the distance he could see a few small farmhouses, smoke curling from their chimneys, neatly set against larger hills in the background that were radiant with the reds and yellows of fall. This was what Only had pictured when he first began contemplations of setting off into the world—these open places to run free. He wandered a few steps into the field, and three grouse were flushed in front of him, their fierce wingbeats nearly scaring him out of his wits. A large butterfly fluttered overhead, and Only leaped for it just for fun. Then he bolted into a gallop, zig zagging at random, stretching his muscles, bounding happily through the glorious countryside. He must have run a mile or more, then stopped to catch his breath. He found a thin babbling brook and lapped at its clear sweet water. Farther on, he entered a field with short green grass and trotted across it to a little rise and from its height was startled to find himself staring down at a herd of pecular-looking animals, the likes of which he had never seen before, but the sight of which again stirred something deep within him.

They were creatures of about his own size, fluffy-white with black hooves and they were grazing contentedly on the grass. They looked docile enough, but Only felt his heartbeat quicken as he trotted down the slope to get a closer look. One of the animals must have seen him because it raised its head and let out an odd sound. The others stopped their grazing and began to huddle close together, facing him as he approached.

There were nearly a hundred of the animals, and they all had their eyes fixed on Only. About ten yards away he stopped and sniffed the air, catching a whiff of collective anxiety from this strange flock of creatures. It was uncomfortable and odd, standing out in the open with all those suspicious eyes looking at him. He took a few more tentative steps toward the animals, but they stood their ground. He got within perhaps five feet of them, drawn by the most peculiar sensation that he ought to *do* something, though he had no idea what. The feeling persisted and became stronger, as he faced them in a kind of Mexican standoff. Deep in his bones he sensed that these weird animals were somehow wrapped up in his own long-forgotten destiny. He took one more deliberate, unsure step forward. Suddenly the largest of the creatures stepped forward as well, and the others behind him began to emit unsettling high-pitched sounds. Only began moving around the herd, keeping a wide berth and watching them. But just as he moved, they turned, too, always facing him. The impulse that he really ought to do *something* continued to needle Only, so he did the first thing that came into his mind. He barked. At this, the animals stopped their baaing and braying and fell silent, staring at him as though he were some kind of curiosity.

Then the large animal who had first stepped out began to approach Only, its head lowered, its eyes staring straight at him. Instantly it came to him that he was vastly outnumbered and hadn't the foggiest idea what they had in mind. Perhaps they were aggressive. He didn't like the odds. He barked again, but the large animal continued forward until it was just a foot or so away from Only, still staring him down; then it craned its neck out toward him and let out a loud *baa* right in his face. At this, the other animals began to crowd in closer behind their leader. Only tensed for a second; then, in one of his least proud moments, he bolted off in the opposite direction like the proverbial bat out of hell. Such was his first encounter with the intended purpose of his breed.

"Oh, George," Alice said sorrowfully, "what *are* we going to do?"

George removed his glasses and began wiping them on his shirt. They were sitting in the living room of the old house. The girls were upstairs, playing. "I don't think there's anything right now," he said.

"But it's been a whole week," she said.

"We've done everything we can," he said. "The pound doesn't have him, nobody's answered the ads in the papers, nobody's seen him in the neighborhood. We've spent all the time we could driving around. It's just a wait-and-see right now."

"I just hope that if he's been stolen they give him a nice home," Alice said.

"Well, if he gets away he'll probably come back."

"But if he's stolen they could have taken him anywhere. They could have taken him to the West Coast."

"He'd probably like it out there. Get himself in the movies or something."

"Oh please, don't joke," she said, "not now."

"I'd better be going," he said and stood up.

"I think we've gone down every street within miles. If he was run over, we'd have found him, don't you think?" she asked.

"I'd think so, yes." He put on his coat and went to the door.

"George," she said, "what do you suppose made him leave?"

He looked at her curiously. "I never knew what made him do anything," he said. "Always had a mind of his own."

"I think it might have been us."

"What does *that* mean?"

"That we've split up. This was his home and now its broken. It hasn't been the same since . . ."

"I know," he said. "I'll talk to you tomorrow."

Only spent the night under the stars at the edge of a large field. He had traveled quite a distance that day after his run-in with the sheep and was settled on a grassy knoll as a golden harvest moon rose above the eastern hills and crept silently across the sky, bathing him in its light. He slept soundly, though, and dreamed peaceful dreams.

All the next day and the next he made his way alternately through farm lands and little wooded spots. Hunger was beginning to gnaw him again. One morning he approached a small farmhouse hoping to find something to eat, but the farmer hurled a stone at him and chased him away. That same afternoon great storm clouds began to billow in from the north. There was a briskness in the air that soon turned to bitter cold, and by sundown small flakes of snow began to fall. Only had been moving along a ridge and as the snow piled up he found himself overcome by a desire to stop this wandering for a while. It was beginning to seem aimless. Just how big was this human world? he wondered. The warmth of home seemed far away.

As light faded toward darkness and the snow continued to hiss through the trees, he could see ahead of him and below the lights of a tiny village with smoke curling from a dozen or so chimneys. Nestled in a small valley by the side of a hill, the village twinkled like a scene from a fairytale.

Only made his way off the ridge and down to a narrow road. He padded cautiously past the first few houses; not a sign of life stirred outside of them but their windows glowed jack-o'-lantern-like, warm and happy-looking. He trotted down to the main section of the village, where there was a little square, not unlike his own park back in Wimbeldon. It had big trees and an old cannon and a white, tall-steepled little church on one side of it. There were also two or three small stores, but they were dark and closed. Only padded through the snow across the park and wandered near several houses from which the wonderful aromas of food wafted deliciously into the air. He stood beneath a kitchen window and raised his nose into the air, his back and head caked with snow. He thought about crawling under the house, but there seemed no place to get through so he continued on, leaving the square and stores and houses behind.

Not so far down the road was another house, a tiny little house, square and neat, with a flagpole in front. A short distance away there was a larger house, and Only again smelled rich aromas of someone's cooking. It smelled like pot roast, which brought back painful memories. He meandered around that house and stood beneath its kitchen window; inside he could hear a voice talking faintly, a strange voice, older-sounding, occasionally answered by a much younger-sounding female voice. Only walked to the back of the house, looking for garbage cans, but there were none.

Then some distance beyond he saw a small shed-like structure, unpainted and ramshackle, but it seemed unoccupied. He plodded over to it and noticed an oddly familiar smell. There was a door, but he managed to nose it open and walked in. In the dark he could barely see, but the floor was covered with straw, and there were rows of boxes set up high. The place couldn't have been more than ten feet long by five feet wide, almost like a little box, and in the dark he sensed that some other living thing was in there with him. No sooner had that sensation struck him than something high in one of the boxes emitted a loud and frightened *squawk,* and this was followed by more squawks from other boxes. He lifted his head and saw a large bird with a hooked beak and reddish substance atop its head and two beady eyes glaring down at him. Only grunted and looked around, trying to adjust to the dim light. The bird reminded him somewhat of the duck back in the forest, and he tucked a malicious thought away in his mind and explored the rest of the tiny shack. What kept coming back to him was the smell of the place, as though he had been there before, in some distant part of his life, the sweet smell of straw and a few corn cobs scattered around, picked bone-clean. Wet and shivering from the cold, hungry and tired, Only thrashed around in the thin layer of straw and lay down, his head between his paws. At least he was out of the snow. All through the night the birds in their boxes above him seemed agitated and every so often would let out a squawk, but after a while he drifted off to sleep. Visions of pot roast and a warm fireside and the sanctity of his garden filled his dreams.

Morning light filtered through cracks in the sides of the little chicken coop, but Only lay unmoving in his nest of hay. Hunger was rolling around in him like a BB in a bathtub. He was starting to have doubts about this great adventure of his. At the beginning he had somehow assumed that things like food and shelter and protection would be miraculously taken care of as they always had. Not in his faintest thoughts had he believed he could be without. The experience was not pleasant. In the pit of his empty stomach he wondered if he could ever find his way home again. If he did, he was certain he would be punished, because he knew what he had done was wrong. But at this point he would be willing to take whatever was dished out.

He heard a muffled sound outside, and the door to the coop swung open on rusty hinges. A human figure was silhouetted against the bright morning sun and loomed large in the doorway. It was a man's figure, tall and gaunt, with a slouch hat and long arms and legs, carrying a walking stick. Only jumped to his feet and backed into a corner.

"Hey!" the man cried. "What's this!"

Only cringed against the wood boards of the henhouse, feeling guilty and afraid. He felt cornered because the man was blocking the lone exit. Only was certain he was going to be caned.

The man craned his neck forward and cautiously entered the coop, inspecting the roosts. Only saw his chance to bolt out and was about to make a getaway when the man turned to him.

"Come in to get out of the cold, did you?" he said gently. He bent down and beckoned Only to him. "Come on," he said. "Well, come on over here." He was holding out his hand. The voice was a kind voice, older, raspy, but without malice. It reminded Only of Dobie at Dr. Peltz's office.

Slowly, Only straightened himself up and stood looking at the stranger.

"Come 'ere," the man commanded, and Only padded over to him. The hand was still outstretched, and when Only got close enough the man patted him on the head.

"Now where'd you come from?" he said. "Lookee here, you been in some kind of scrape, haven't you?" He gingerly lifted Only's torn ear and examined it, then peered at the gash on his nose. "You wait for a minute, you hear?" the man said. He rose up and reached under one of the birds in its box. The bird squawked, but the man retrieved a brown oval object and put it in a little bag he was carrying. He did this twice more, then looked at Only and went to two more of the birds and retrieved eggs from them too.

"C'mon with me," the man said, walking to the door. Only wavered briefly, but there was something trustworthy in the man's tone that put him at ease. He followed him out into the snow.

A single set of human footprints led to the coop, not from the large house, but from the tiny square shack with the flagpole in front. Only noticed that a flag was now flying from the pole. They followed the tracks to the little house, and the man opened the door. There was one small room with a single lightbulb dangling from the ceiling and a cot in a corner, neatly made, and a chair next to it and a table and a little stove and an icebox. Only noticed the icebox first, because he knew that was where food was kept.

The man went to a sink and turned on a faucet and filled a bowl with water and put it on the floor, beckoning Only to it. He sniffed the water but didn't drink, for he had had his fill of water from the snow. But he looked plaintively up at the man and went to the icebox and let out a tiny whimper.

"Oh, that's it, eh?" the man said. "Figured that. But you'll have to wait a minute or two."

It wasn't long before the smells of bacon and eggs and toasted bread filled the little room. The man was working hard over the stove and within a few minutes he had prepared a plate of food for himself and a bowl for Only: eggs and bacon and toast all mushed together. Only gobbled it up so fast the man began to chuckle.

"You really were hungry, weren't you ole feller?" Only waddled over to him and got another pat on the head. "Well, here's a little more for you." He put down the plate he'd been eating from, and Only licked up the scraps greedily.

Just as he finished, there was the sound of a vehicle stopping outside, and the man got up and opened a door that led into another part of the small house. This room was even plainer than the other; it had a counter and a stool and a row of small boxes. It was barely as large as the bathroom back in Wimbeldon.

The man opened the door and let another man in who was carrying a big cloth bundle and he reached in and handed a packet of letters to the first man, then peered at Only, who was standing in the doorway that led to the back room.

"What you got there, Jake?" the new man asked.

"Found him in the henhouse this morning. Guess he got in there during the night to get out of the cold."

"That's one of them—what you call 'em? Cain't remember the name now. Seen 'em on the television sometimes, in advertisements."

"Yea, I forget too," Jake said. "Probably strayed off from someplace. Ain't got a collar or anything. Been in a fight or somethin', cause he's all bit up. Half-starved too."

"What you gonna do with him?" the other asked.

"Dunno," Jake said. "Reckon I cain't turn him out. Not right now anyhow. Ain't decided yet."

"Lord have mercy, Jake, you keep him, he'll eat you out of house and home, a dog that size."

Jake shrugged, "Ain't much of a house or home to eat me out of, I'd say."

The other man laughed. "Guess you're right. Well, I'd best get on my way. Snow's got me behind schedule. You need anything?"

"You can get me some stamps," Jake said. "About ten sheets of thirteens and some tens and, let's see, 'bout a dozen or so of them big brown envelopes. Ole Mrs. Horner's been sending all sorts of things to her sister down to Hartford. Plum ran me out of package envelopes."

"I'll bring 'em up tomorrow," the other man said. "Good luck with . . . guess you ain't got a name for that, have you?"

"Nope," Jake said, "I asked him, but he didn't say nothing."

"Least you know it's a *him.*"

"Yep," Jake said slyly. "I looked."

Eleven

J AKE SPENT THE NEXT HALF HOUR SORTING OUT THE
packet of mail the other man had left him, while
Only lay curled up in a corner watching. Then he
went into the back room and began lacing on thick
rubber boots and put on a heavy coat and a blue hat
with a bill on it. He put the sorted mail in a bag,
slung it over his shoulder and went to the door.

"You wanna go for a little walk?" Jake asked. He
held open the door, and Only got up and went
outside. They walked toward the village through the
snow, Only trotting alongside. Then Jake stopped at
a mailbox in front of a house and deposited several
letters, then walked up to the porch and tossed a
newspaper near the door. He did this at three or four
houses on the way to the village and at practically
every house in the village itself. Two or three times
people in the houses came out and the first thing
they asked about was Only.

"Where on earth, Jake?"

"What is it?"

"You going to keep him?"

"How come he ain't got no tail?"

"Looks like some kind of bear . . ."

Then they walked out of the village down a long winding country road, slippery with ice, up a hill and down another, desolate land with bleak forest on all sides. After about two miles they came upon a lone farmhouse where Jake put some letters in the mailbox and threw his last paper onto the front porch.

"Okay," he said, looking down at Only. "That's all for today, we can go home now."

They walked back through the village, and Jake stopped at a small store where several men sat inside, warming themselves around a black pot-bellied stove in a corner. Only followed Jake inside.

"Great Scot!" one of the men cried when Only padded toward him. He was smoking a pipe and nearly dropped it out of his mouth. Jake told his attentive audience about finding Only in the hen-house.

"I s'pose he belongs to somebody, but I'm darned if I can imagine who," he said. "Ain't nobody 'round here got any dog like that."

"You could put an ad in the paper," one of them suggested.

"Intend to," Jake said. "Gonna call them right now." He went to a phone on the wall and dialed a number, while Only was being petted and fussed over by the men in the store. One of them went behind a counter and returned with a piece of sausage and thrust it at Only, who munched it out of his hand. This was more like what he'd expected when he left home, not the hostile and uncaring world he'd seen before he got here.

They left the store after a while and made their way back to Jake's shack, but instead of going inside, Jake led Only to the larger house next door. He didn't knock, but went right inside, Only following him.

"Annie," he called out, "I got a surprise for you."

An older woman appeared from a doorway toward the back of the house and when she saw Only she let out a cry of disapproval.

"What is *that?*" she demanded.

"It's a big old dog," Jake said. "What'd you think it was?"

"Get it out of here," Annie said. "I don't want no dogs inside my house. Dogs belong outside."

"Aw, Annie," Jake protested, "he's just lost or somethin'. Found him in the henhouse this morning. He was—"

"Henhouse!" she shouted. "That great big thing was in my henhouse! My Lord, it's a wonder any of the chickens are still alive!"

"He wouldn't harm a fly," Jake said. "Gentle kind of dog, I think. He just went in there to get out of the cold."

"You get him out of here right now, Jake," she said. "This instant."

"Aw, Annie, I didn't bring him over here to see you anyway. I brought him to see Elsie."

"Well she's not here yet. Hasn't come home from school. And he's not going to come in here smelling up my place and—ah! lookit, he's tracked in all that mud and water on my floors."

Only sensed the unfriendliness of the woman, Annie, and shrank back a little and even tried to look forlorn. It didn't help.

"Out!" she said, pointing to the door.

"Annie," Jake grumbled, "if I didn't know we were born in the same family, I'd swear you weren't any sister of mine."

"An you're an old fool, Jake," she retorted, "bringing something like that in here."

Jake was standing in the door, letting Only slink out past him. "You tell Elsie to come see me when she gets home, hear?"

Annie scowled, but nodded. "And don't be bringing him over here on Sunday either," she said. "He can stay outside, but he's not coming in."

"Sometimes I think you ain't got a good heart," Jake said. An indecipherable invective was hurled as Jake shut the door.

They had been back in Jake's little room for about an hour when there was a faint knock at the door. Jake opened it, and standing there in a long cloth coat and hat was a girl. Only perked up. The first thing he noticed was her eyes. They were amazingly large and bright greenish-blue. Her face was very fair, and when she took off her cap, long, golden-blond hair fell down to her shoulders.

"Hi, Uncle Jake," she said.

"Well, c'mon in, there, Elsie. I got somebody I want you to meet."

"Aunt Annie said you got a dog," Elsie said. Then, as she looked past Jake and saw Only lying there on the floor, she cried out happily and rushed over to him, kneeling and petting him. "Oh, it's beautiful," she said. "It's so fluffy!"

"It's a *him*," Jake said. He told her the story of Only's arrival. Only was delighted at the affection being lavished upon him. It seemed like so long since anyone had paid him any attention. He licked contentedly at Elsie's small hands as she stroked him gently.

"I had to put an ad in the paper," Jake told her, "so I don't know how long he's gonna be here. I know somebody must be looking for him."

"Oh, I hope not," Elsie said. "I hope not."

That was how it came that Only found a new family.

The ad Jake placed ran for three weeks in the county newspaper that he delivered to supplement his postal route. There was no response. In the intervening time, Only was made to feel at home, with the exception of Annie, who kept him at bay and refused to let him inside her house. Each day Only would accompany Jake on his rounds and he soon learned that Jake made his deliveries six days a week and that on Sunday he did not, but went to Annie's house for dinner in the afternoon and usually stayed till well after dark. Only lived in the chicken coop. Jake had persuaded Annie that it would be a good thing.

"He'll keep out the weasels and rats," Jake argued. Reluctantly Annie conceded this was true and in time she even warmed to him a bit but still wouldn't let him inside her house.

A kind of live-and-let-live attitude developed between Only and the chickens. At first they gave him a wide berth, but soon figured out that he meant them no harm. Once, in fact, a weasel did try to get into the coop but it took one look at Only and scampered off.

Weeks went by, and each day beautiful Elsie came in the late afternoon to play with Only. They would romp outside if the weather was good, and when it wasn't she would come into the coop and sit with him for long hours, or visit him in Jake's room. For those three weeks that the advertisement ran in the lost and found of the newspaper, Only was in a kind of limbo. Jake noticed Elsie's growing affection and occasionally warned her that somebody might well come one day and claim Only, so she'd better not get too set on his always being there. Also a part of this limbo was that nobody knew what Only's name was, and since it was uncertain how long he'd be there, he was called by no name. Instead, they would just say, "Here, boy," or, "C'mon, fella." But Only didn't mind. Actually, it was something of a relief to him not to have to answer to "Only." It gave him a new identity. An identity of his own.

One day when they were making the rounds, Jake accidently dropped a newspaper while he was putting mail in a box. Only nosed at it and then gingerly picked it up in his teeth. He looked up at Jake, who was still sorting through the mail, and suddenly Only was struck with a bright idea. He trotted up the walk to the house and deposited the newspaper at the front door, then proudly turned to Jake. The old man's mouth had dropped open in disbelief.

"Well, I'll be," he cried. "I'll be!" Only received a pat on his head.

At the next place Jake put the mail in the box and then handed a newspaper to Only, who took it in his mouth and looked up at Jake for a moment. Jake motioned him toward the house, so Only ran up and left the paper on the porch. Jake was delighted.

"You ain't as dumb as you look," was his observation. He patted Only on the head again, and thereafter, at each house, Only received a paper and put it where he had seen Jake leave it. It made Only feel good to do this, to be useful in some way.

More weeks passed and Only had settled relatively happily into his new life. Sometimes he thought about Alice and George and the girls and his garden and the cat, but they were memories fading and blurred, like old photographs frozen in time. He had never intended to leave Wimbeldon for good, but somehow life here was simpler and easier to deal with. He had grown terribly fond of Jake and Elsie; it was almost like the old days back home, before the children, before the split-up. . . .

His routine was the same each day, but he always looked forward to it. In the morning he would meet Jake in front of the little post office shack, and they would deliver the mail and the papers, then in the afternoons Elsie would come play with him. Sundays they would go to Annie's, and he would sit on the porch, but Elsie would be there, too, and there were always good scraps from the table afterward. The single thing that threw Only off was holidays.

Thanksgiving was the first. He had gone out to meet Jake, but Jake wasn't there. He thought he might have been late and missed him, but just as he was about to start out on his own to catch up, Jake appeared on the porch of Annie's house and called for him to come over. That day he got a wonderful portion of scraps from a big Thanksgiving dinner.

One morning not too many weeks later, Only went to Jake's at the appointed time but found no one there. He waited for a while, then walked around to the front and when he still didn't see Jake, he took off down the little road, thinking he probably had missed him somehow. There was a fresh snow on the ground, and the sky was overcast. At the first house, Only trotted up to the porch, but there was no newspaper there, or at the second or the third. He was bewildered. It couldn't be Sunday, because they had just had Sunday—at least he thought they had—a few days earlier.

He continued into the village, but the stores were closed. He could see people in their houses, and there was an atmosphere of gaity and reverence and joy in the air, but no newspapers and no Jake. Finally at one house he saw two children playing in the snow on a bright new sled, and a proud father and mother standing by watching them. Only wandered up and was greeted with hugs and squeals from the children, two little girls who reminded him of Kimberly and Caroline, and for some reason the couple turned his thoughts back to Alice and George in the days when they were all a family. A flash of bittersweet nostaliga swept over Only. he stayed and romped with the children for a little while and then meandered off, but instead of heading back to his chicken coop, he turned down a narrow country lane and strayed off into some woods.

All was quiet except for the crunch of the snow beneath his paws. He wandered aimlessly through this forest, deep in thought, prickled by an urge to know what was happening back home. He felt happy here in the village, and he had come to love Jake and Elsie, but something also told him he belonged with Alice and the children and George, even in their confusing lifestyle. A rabbit burst from a thicket of underbrush and scampered off through the snow, but Only paid it no attention. He stopped after a while and lifted his head to savor the smells of the winter forest. It was nice here, being able to roam as he wished and come and go as he pleased. He could have chased that rabbit if he'd wanted to, and for as long as he wanted to; it just hadn't appealed to him then. Someday, he thought, he would have to make a decision, but for now he'd let things drift along as they were.

At the same time Only was wandering in the forest, his name and his memory crept into a conversation more than one hundred miles away at the Christmas dinner table of George and Alice Martin, back in Wimbeldon. They had excused the girls from the table to go play with their Christmas presents, and George and Alice sat across from each other sipping wine.

"You know, I can't help it," Alice said. "I still think about him two or three times a day."

George nodded solemnly. "It's hard to figure out," he said. "Nothing. Not a sign. I think if he'd been run over or anything like that we'd have surely heard."

"He must have been stolen," she said. "But I can't imagine the kind of people who'd steal a dog would keep it themselves—they'd probably sell it, so maybe he's got a good home somewhere."

"Let's hope so," George said. He was gazing absently out the window.

"Every once in a while," Alice said joylessly, "I think I hear him scratching at the door to the garden to get in."

George turned and looked at her directly. He could see the sorrow in her eyes, and he felt it himself. But he also felt he had to be practical, for he was, above all else, a practical man.

"He's not coming back, you know. I think we have to face that."

"He might," she said defensively.

"Slim chance."

"Better than none."

"I suppose," he said, "but after all, it's been three months."

Alice sighed. "I guess you're right, but . . . well, things just seem so different without him. The house just isn't the same . . ."

George nodded and took a sip of wine and began packing his pipe. He looked at his watch and started to get up. "I think I'll go up and say goodby to the girls," he said, "and head on back."

Alice smiled ruefully, pushed her chair away from the table, stood up and started clearing the dishes.

"Want some help?" he asked.

"No, you go ahead up and see the girls. I'll finish this."

George returned in about fifteen minutes and found Alice washing dishes in the kitchen sink. "I'd better be going," he said. "The dinner was wonderful—I'm glad we did it."

"Would you like a drink? A glass of brandy or something?"

"I don't think so," he said. He had his jacket in his hand and began putting it on. Alice turned off the water and dried her hands on a towel. She marched up to him and took him by both wrists.

"George," she said, "why don't you stay here tonight?"

He looked at her curiously and painfully. "Why?" he asked.

"Because I want you to, dummy, that's why."

"Well, maybe I'll have one more drink. Maybe that glass of brandy."

"Why not have two?" she said. "Or three."

"Maybe I will," he said.

"Good," she said seductively.

Twelve

Two more Christmases passed, and the summers, autumns and springs in between found Only content, more or less, with Jake and Elsie in the little village. He had become something of a fixture there, delivering his papers and toddling along after Jake, or romping with Elsie in the afternoons or sometimes just wandering around by himself through the streets or in the woods. He had become reasonably self-sufficient, living in his henhouse with the chickens and protecting them from the weasels, skunks and rats. Even old Annie had gotten to like him, although he was still not allowed in her house.

But something else was happening to Only that he just barely perceived. He seemed to be slowing down. He wasn't as frisky as he once was, and he became more content to sleep and lie around. The boundless energy was slipping away, his eyesight was poorer than it was once, his hearing a little off and he got the rheumatism sometimes when the weather was bad, though it didn't amount to much.

One morning a great storm blew out of the north. It was mid-February, the most desolate and grim time of year, and blue-black clouds hung malevolently over the hills around the village, and a savage wind whistled around eaves and shutters and shrieked through the boards of the henhouse. The snow began to blow in swirling, blinding sheets, and by midday there was more than a foot of it. Only had gone to meet Jake as usual but was let inside the little shack and given a snack to eat and he could see that Jake wasn't dressed to make his rounds. A little while later, Elsie knocked at the door.

"They let us out from school early today, Uncle Jake," she said. "This storm's supposed to be real bad." Only had gotten up and walked over to her and put his head in her lap to be scratched.

"It does look like a big 'un," Jake said, "but seems to me it's letting up some." He was looking out the window.

They sat there for another hour talking quietly and sipping some hot tea Jake had brewed. Two or three times Jake got up and took a look outside and the last time he said, "Well, the worst of it seems to be over now," and he began putting on his boots. Only jumped up immediately and began to pad about the little place in excitement.

"Can I go with you today, Uncle Jake?" Elsie asked.

"Oh, child, I don't think you'd like it. It's going to get really, really cold out there."

"I'm dressed for it," she said. "I think it'd be fun."

"Suit yourself then. But I don't want to hear any whining when we're way out by the Marston place, and it's ten below zero, and we've got to walk all the way back with the wind in our faces," he said good-naturedly.

Elsie smiled broadly and began putting on her heavy coat, while Jake got his mail pouch from the other room.

It had stopped snowing entirely when the three of them walked out into the dim light, but the snow clouds still layered ominously over the white-covered mountains. By the time they reached the second house, flakes again began to fall, and by the time they got to the village it had started coming down heavily again.

"You sure you don't want to wait for me here in the store while Only and I go up to the Marstons'?" Jake asked.

"Oh, I'll go," Elsie said. "It isn't all that far."

"Suit yourself," Jake said again.

The long winding road to the Marstons' was blanketed much more heavily than Jake had expected, and there were times when the road became completely invisible beneath the snow. There also were treacherous patches of ice under the snow, but the three of them plodded on, with Only bounding in front, up to his chest sometimes in the soft white powder.

"Neither rain nor snow nor sleet nor dark of night," Jake was saying grandly, "shall keep them from their appointed rounds."

It was almost dark when they reached the Marston place. Jake gave Only a paper, the last one, while he put a few letters in the mailbox. The snow had begun to fall in torrents, swirling silently and evilly around them in the failing light, and they could see no more than a few feet ahead.

"We'd best hurry up," Jake said. "I don't much like the looks of this." The wind blew through their clothing and even through Only's shaggy coat of fur—he was shivering despite the exertion of plodding and bounding through the thick snowfall. Then without warning Elsie let out a shriek and sank nearly out of sight. She was just a few feet from Jake, who thrashed his way over to her and grabbed her extended hand.

"Oh, it's freezing," she cried out.

"That must be the stream," Jake said in a grim and worried voice. "Means we're off the road." He lifted her out and felt her trousers. "You're soaking," he said. "We've got to hurry now before it freezes and you get the frostbite." Only was standing almost neck-deep in a drift, watching as Jake led Elsie by the hand. They made their way painfully for perhaps a quarter of a mile, but kept falling off into ruts and depressions in the ground. They faltered on the slip-and-stumble trek through the darkness and the blizzard, and Only sensed the edge of fear in Jake's voice when he said, "I think we've got to try to take a shortcut, through the woods here. It's just taking too long trying to keep to the road."

Only followed close behind as Jake led Elsie into the woods.

"It'll be more than a mile to the village by the road, but I think we can cut that by half going this way," he said. "But watch for stumps and things. Elsie, do you feel all right?"

"I'm cold, Uncle Jake," she said.

"I know, child. I am, too, a little bit. But we haven't that far to go."

The crack came without any warning, like a gigantic pair of trousers being ripped in the black, snow-filled sky above them, and the huge limb was sheared off at its base from the trunk of a tree by the heavy weight of the snow. Only heard it first and reacted by bolting backward as it fell directly in front of Elsie and directly on top of Jake. He let out a groan from beneath the tangled branches, and Elsie cried out in fright. She thrashed her way to where Jake lay. All that was visible was his head. Only had come to her side and in the faint light could see that Jake's face was contorted into a mask of pain.

"My leg," he cried pitifully. "I think it's broke. I can't feel anything."

"Oh, Uncle Jake! Oh, Uncle Jake!" she wailed.

"Go on," he said. "Go on straight through. The village can't be that far—you'll probably come out around the Turners' place somewhere. Get them to send somebody back."

"Oh, Uncle Jake," Elsie said again, her voice pitched above the screaming wind. "I don't know. I don't want to go alone."

"Ah," he said. "You've got to! You'll freeze to death in half an hour, and so will I if you don't get help. Take the dog. He'll probably be able to find the way back," Jake said, motioning toward Only with a grimace.

"Oh, Uncle Jake. I'm scared," she whimpered.

"You have to do it," he shouted. "Hurry. There isn't much time!"

Elsie, tears already frozen on her cheeks, started out. Only's instinct was to go with her, but he didn't want to leave Jake either.

"Go on!" Jake motioned to him. "Go on after her. Show her the way!" And so Only took out after Elsie, leaping in the darkened snowdrifts, trying to catch her scent or hear her movements above the howling wind.

He caught up with her without too much trouble, but getting free of the forest wasn't as simple as Jake made it sound. The blizzard was still blinding, limiting visibility to a few feet, and as Elsie struggled through brambles and brown wintered underbrush,

Only got the impression they might be going in a circle. Worse, he had no more idea where they were or how to get out of the woods than she did.

They had been moving at a nightmare crawl for what seemed like a long time, when Elsie suddenly dropped to her hands and knees, sinking into the soft snow and weeping.

"I don't know where we're going," she cried. "Poor Uncle Jake . . ." Only nosed up to her, and she threw her arms around his neck. He could feel her cheek with his nose, and it was cold and briny. "I'm so tired," she said. "I have to rest for a few minutes." Only hunkered down next to her, and she held tightly to him. "You're so warm," she sobbed. They lay that way, next to each other for a long while; then Only slowly rose up and sniffed at the fierce wind. He had caught a whiff of Jake's scent, off to his right. He wished he could have found some way to tell Elsie what he was thinking, but since that was impossible, he simply looked at her and shook the snow from his coat and began plodding in the direction from which Jake's odor had wafted. He found him, not far away, still pinned under the enormous limb. They had gotten less than a hundred yards in all that time.

Jake was in terrible pain and was startled when Only appeared out of the blizzard.

"Where's Elsie?" he shouted, almost as if he expected an answer. Only nudged close into Jake, snuggling next to him, and Jake, somehow sensing what was happening, put his arms around Only, taking his life-giving warmth, breathing heavily and desperately. After a while Only rose up again. Jake at first tried to tug him back down, but then, even through his pain, must have somehow realized that Elsie was nearby, because he let go of Only, and Only plowed and struggled his way back to the spot where Elsie lay.

The blizzard howled monstrously all through the night, and the snow continued to pile upon them there in the forest. And all through the night Only made his treks back and forth between Jake and Elsie, sharing the warmth of his body and fur with one, then the other. Sometime just before dawn, the blackest and most miserable time of all, Only was lying with Jake and felt a strange, slackening sensation from his injured friend. He licked Jake's cheeks with his warm tongue, but the grizzled face was serene, its eyes closed. A wave of horrible fear swept over Only, and he poked Jake hard with his snout but could not seem to wake him up. He whimpered and pawed him and snuggled as close as he could, but Jake was as still as a figurine under glass. Only stayed with him as long as he dared, then pulled away to go back to Elsie. He found her lying still, too, but when he nudged her she opened her eyes, and he crawled down beside her until she seemed warm again.

The storm had calmed somewhat when the first dim light began to glow behind the eastern hills.

Elsie got to her feet and half staggering, half trudging, began to walk. Only was again torn between going back to Jake or accompanying Elsie, but he went with her, because it seemed likely they would find someone to help them now that it was getting light. The two of them fought their way through the forest in snow that sometimes reached as high as Elsie's waist and was completely over Only's head, so that he had to leap forward, froglike, his head raised as high as it would go, and bull his way through it. They reached the edge of the forest and saw what appeared to be a large field and plowed across it. Elsie let out a sigh of joy, for in the distance she could see a farmhouse.

Most of the rest happened in a blur from the moment Elsie spied the farmhouse until they reached it, from the confused and desperate conversation inside and the rushing around and the arrival of some men in a weird vehicle with large wheels, into which Elsie and Only were placed, until the time the vehicle stopped somewhere in the cold icy morning, and Elsie pointed, and Only was let out and at first followed, then led, the men as they struggled their way through the banks of snow in the forest, and then reaching the spot where Jake lay under the big limb and the men rooting around under the snow and finally uncovering his face, blue and waxy but still somehow serene, and then pulling the limb off and the men picking Jake up with Only plowing alongside as they lifted him in an eerie little procession out of the forest and Elsie's shrieks and horrible cries and sobs as they put Jake in the back of the vehicle and driving to the village and then to Annie's place. This time Only was let inside, but everyone seemed too distressed and preoccupied to pay him any attention, and so after a while he stood by the door and whimpered and scratched, and somebody let him out, and he went to Jake's place and scratched at the door there. When there was no answer, Only slowly made his way back to his chicken coop, exhausted and bewildered and scared.

Thirteen

〜⌒〜

IT WAS MORE THAN A WEEK BEFORE THEY BURIED JAKE.
The snow was so deep and the ground so hard that
gravedigging was almost impossible.

Only knew, and yet he didn't know.

It was his first encounter with mortality, except
for the duck that he had killed in the forest, and
that of course had been different. There was a wake
that lasted nearly the whole week. The village had
no funeral parlor, so they dressed Jake up in his one
good suit and laid him out in Annie's parlor in a
pine box, and people from the village were constantly coming and going from early morning till
late in the evening. Then one bright but cheerless
morning, they took Jake away in the back of the
same truck that had found him in the woods. Annie
and Elsie rode in someone else's car, and Only was
let up into the back of the truck with Jake as they
drove to the little white steepled church on the
square.

The cold winter wind tore at Only's fur as he stood watch over his friend, thinking that he somehow might just pop up out of the box and things would go back to how they had been. But a dark, hurting, mournful cloud tore away at this hope, and when they got to the church Only was allowed inside and sat with Elsie and Annie while the preacher said his piece. The gatherers sang hymns, and then they loaded Jake back on the truck and drove to a little hill not far from the village square. When they slid the box off the truck, Only felt an impulse to stop them, for he knew this somehow signified an end of sorts. For a few moments he simply stood there, not growling or showing any outward sign of hostility, but his staunch, bristling figure, feet planted in the back of the truck, was menacing, and one of the people who was trying to get a hand on the box called for Elsie, and she came over, tears brimming, and took Only by the fur on his back of his neck and gently helped him down, and he waddled alongside her to a spot where the frozen earth was freshly dug and where a few pitiful flowers had been placed and everyone else had gathered. More intonations were raised, and then several men with ropes lowered the box into the hole, and Annie and Elsie each took a handful of the cold dirt and tossed it into the grave and then walked away followed by most of the others.

Only watched them, forlorn and desperate. He barked, hoping they might come back, but Elsie turned her head just once and then continued on. The few remaining men began to shovel dirt into the hole while Only looked on helplessly. When they were finished they took their shovels and left him there alone in the cold February sun.

Only waited for a while by the graveside and then he went over to the mound and pawed at it, but something told him it was hopeless. Nonetheless, he stayed there all that day and through the night too. Elsie was worried about him, but Annie had told her he'd come home when he was ready, and so they let him be. But the following afternoon when Elsie got home from school Only was still nowhere in sight, and she bundled up and walked through the village to the little graveyard and found him there, sitting on his haunches over the mound of dirt. She knelt in front of him and put her arms around his neck and began to cry softly, and he licked her face, and when she finally got up and began coaxing him to come with her, he realized that it was over and he waddled sadly after her, not looking back, trying to think of other things.

Things slowly began to change in the village. Not long after Jake died, some people came and began removing the stuff from the front of the little square shack. They even took down the flagpole, and once when Only was down in the village he noticed it had reappeared in front of a new brick building. Every day for a while he followed the old route that he and Jake had taken so many times. To his dismay, he observed one day a man driving a small car slow down and toss newspapers at the houses where he once had delivered them by mouth. The new postman seemed cool and distant to Only.

The winter thawed to an early spring, and the days became longer, but for Only it wasn't the same anymore. He hung around his chicken coop most of the day until Elsie came home. Sometimes Annie let him into the house, usually on Sundays and mostly as a concession to Elsie, but he didn't much feel welcome there. Jake's old shack lay boarded up and abandoned, a constant and bitter reminder of happier times. More and more during the lengthening days Only began to think of his old home back in Wimbeldon. Sometimes he felt guilty for ever leaving, sometimes he simply thought fondly of his garden and occasionally wondered about the cat. And he also thought of Blossom in a longing and bittersweet way.

His rheumatism had been acting up for several days, and nearly a week of spring rains kept him cooped up in the henhouse like one of the chickens. All during this time something was working inside him, a voice or calling that beckoned him to go back home. At first he ignored it, as he had before, but this time the impulse did not fade.

One afternoon the rain let up, and Elsie called to him from the back door of Annie's house. He rose stiffly and went out of the coop and met her halfway in the backyard. They took a long walk together down a country lane with the leaves dripping and a few little flowers poking out of the ground, violets and daffodils, and the smell was soft and fragrant under the canopy of trees. They walked through the village and past the graveyard on the hill, and Only felt a pang of sorrow that he could feel in Elsie as well. He wished again that he could speak words, because he had something to tell her, but since he knew he couldn't, he could only hope she would understand.

They got to a place where the road took a bend, which was usually where they would turn around and head back home; but this time, when Elsie turned, Only kept on going.

He stopped just before the bend would carry him out of sight and faced her. She called him, but he stood his ground. She called again, but he walked on a few more steps, then turned to her again. Somehow she must have understood because she stopped calling and watched him, and the two of them looked at each other for a long while. The sun seemed to burst in one last flash of brilliance before disappearing behind the hills, and then Only drew in a breath and turned away from Elsie for a last time and he trotted off, a little apprehensively, into the twilight.

He traveled most of that night and the next day by country road. Navigation, he discovered, was going to be a problem, because he had absolutely no idea where he was nor how to get where he was trying to go. The lone clue that came to him was that when he had left Wimbeldon so long ago the morning sun had been on his right and the afternoon sun on his left. So he figured that if he kept it the opposite way now, he would eventually get back. But the winding country roads made this kind of navigation difficult at best, and he was never sure of the accuracy of his course except at sunrise and sunset. Furthermore, overcast days threw him off entirely. But still he plodded on.

Then one day he found a landmark. He was walking by a fenced-in pasture when on a distant hillside he spied a grazing herd of the weird hoofed animals he had never seen before. This time Only couldn't resist the temptation. He crawled through the fence and loped toward them. Just as before, one of the animals sounded a kind of alarm, and the others stopped their grazing and looked up at Only. They made their strange "baa" noises and kept their eyes warily upon him. Only stopped and faced them, and as before, one of the larger ones stepped out and marched deliberately up to him, looking him in the eye.

This time Only took swift and decisive action. He charged the big animal and bowled it over with a shoulder, and it scrambled to its feet and bolted pell-mell back into the herd. Only spent the next half-hour chasing the flock around the pasture, moving it first one way and then the next, until, exhausted and out of breath, he stopped and watched them flee in a bunch and disappear over one of the little hills as the sun set into a crimson sky. With a gleam of satisfaction in his eye he continued on.

He slept in forests and ate grass and carrion and picked at garbage cans along the road. The farther he went the more his thoughts turned to George and Alice and the girls. He began to envision a reunion in which he would not be scolded, but accepted back into the family the way it had been after he had fallen off the boat.

He knew the girls must have grown, for he had watched them grow from their births, but the old life remained a frozen image in his mind: He pictured them all as though they had not changed, and he also pictured himself in that setting as unchanged. Somehow he came to believe that once he got home, the old energy would come back, and the failing eyesight and the rheumatism would go away.

One day he discovered an enormous road with cars and large trucks whizzing down it, and the going was easy along the sides of this road, and there was water to drink from a ditch and bits of cast-away food to be gleaned, so he stuck with it for a number of days, trudging deliberately through the new fresh shoots of green grass and lifting his nose to catch the fragrant aromas of bright flowers. He had left in the autumn and was returning in the spring, but it never occurred to him that by any sense of poetics it should have been just the reverse, because when he left he had been in the spring of his own life and he was returning now in its autumn. Perhaps it was poetic *justice* instead, since Only did things pretty much backward anyway. His mind was wandering aimlessly, as it did now and then, and his concentration was far elsewhere, and so he never saw the big diesel truck bearing down on him from behind until it was too late.

His first sensation was a horrible *crack,* then spinning across ground and then a numbness in his back legs and then a slowly, but sharply, increasing hurt, a great, unbearable pain that began in his hind legs and spread, so that his entire body felt it was afire. He was wild with fright and pain. He couldn't move, but writhed on the ground and howled in anguish. Once or twice in the intervening minutes he must have passed out, but he revived, and the pain was worse than ever, and he craned down to his shattered leg and hip and savagely tried to bite it off. He was faintly aware of someone, a man, standing over him, looking down, but then everything seemed to spin around, and he sank into a blessed oblivion of blackness.

When he awoke again he was in a cage.

The man, a kindly motorist who had seen the truck hit Only, had managed to get him into the back seat of his car and drive him to a veterinarian's office in a little town not too far down the road. The old country vet had been reluctant to accept Only at first, since he was simply just another stray highway casualty, but the motorist insisted that in the name of simple humanity the vet ought not to let a poor dumb animal suffer. The vet suggested putting Only out of his misery, but the motorist offered to pay for the treatment himself, and the vet, shaking his head in resignation, prepared Only for the operating table. When he had shaved off the hair from the damaged leg and examined it closely, he found to his dismay that it was impossibly mangled. Setting it would have been a waste of time or at least a Herculean effort that he wasn't prepared to make, since he had a bunch of sick dairy cattle worth many thousands of dollars that needed treating at a local farm, and he didn't have time for any kind of sophisticated restructuring operation on a dog. With a sigh of resignation, the vet got out an electric saw and cut off Only's leg just above the haunch, pinched off, then clamped the arteries and began the tedious but less difficult task of sewing him up, all the while cursing his luck for now being saddled with an old three-legged stray dog.

In his cage, Only awoke to a duller pain than the unbearable agony he had felt on the highway and he felt sluggish and strange. He nosed around to the place where his left leg had been and felt a shiver of surprise and then horror at the bandaged stump he saw. He tried to gnaw at the bandage to see whether the missing part of the leg was under it but he couldn't get any leverage in the small cage they had put him in. He whimpered all night in fear and hurt, and when the vet appeared next morning at the cage Only growled at him in frustration through the bars of the cage.

The next week or so was a grim and blurred haze of aching and disorientation. Only ate very little, and every once in a while the vet would come and stick a needle in him. It was the most miserable time Only had ever spent in his life: an unrelenting nightmare of pain and fear and loneliness that he could never fully comprehend. Alice and George wouldn't have let this happen to him, he thought; nor Jake nor Elsie. But slowly, with time on his paws, and his thoughts clearer as the wound began to heal, he decided that he had himself to blame for this. He was on his own.

The veterinarian was not an uncompassionate man, but he was a realist when it came to animals, and his realization was simply that even having saved Only's life he could not keep him forever and that unless his owners were found he would have to turn him over to the local pound for, well, "disposal." Once Only was healed enough to get out of the cage, the vet put him in a wire run with a concrete floor until he was satisfied that the bandages could be removed and the stitches could come out. He then placed an advertisement in several newspapers which covered about a fifty-mile radius of his town, reporting a "large English sheepdog, approx. 7 to 9 yrs old, injured by car, please contact Dr. Wm. Walters, High Hill, N.H."

The ad ran for two weeks without response. By this time Only was able to hobble around on three legs and get to the water and food pans at the end of the dog run. Against his better judgment, the vet had actually taken a liking to Only. He was pleased at his resilience and even briefly considered keeping him for himself, but again his sense of practicality ruled that out, and so it was with a keen feeling of reluctance, if not sadness, that he phoned the dog pound one day and told them to come get Only.

Only languished in the pound for nearly two weeks in a crowded dog run with five other dogs of various appearances and dispositions. Most were mongrels, but there was one large, nasty-tempered, shepherd-looking dog who snarled and snapped every time Only got close to him, and so Only found a cool spot in a corner near the back of the run and kept to himself, lying for hours on end, thinking nostalgic thoughts and wondering if he would ever be let out.

Two weeks was about the maximum stay a dog was allowed in the pound. A sour-looking keeper came occasionally and got one of the dogs, and it would not return to the pen, and on a few other occasions people would come and let out whoops of joy and a dog would be removed and go with them. But Only remained unmolested by all of this. Dr. Walters, in a moment of generosity, had extended Only's privilege of remaining alive by continuing to run the ad in the newspapers at his own expense for another week. The other dogs came and went, including the shepherd-looking dog, who snarled and growled to the bitter end.

"George," Alice exclaimed into the phone, "I was just looking through the *Globe* this morning in the lost-and-found section. I don't know why I even did it, but something must have told me to. But there's an ad about an injured sheepdog in a little town up in New Hampshire about an hour or so from here. It says he's seven- to nine- years old—that's about Only's age. It also says 'final notice.'"

Seated at his desk at the bank, George was facing a stern old woman who had arrived with a wad of bank statements, claiming, as she did periodically, that the bank was cheating her.

"What else does it say?" he asked grumpily.

"Nothing. But, well, I just think it's worth the chance."

"Why don't you call them?"

"I am," she said.

That morning the sour old pound keeper came to get Only. His time had run out, and he was not alone.

The keeper had three or four ropes and he singled

out three other dogs and slipped a noose over their necks and then he came for Only, who was lying in his corner.

With the other dogs in tow, tangled and yapping, the keeper put a noose over Only's neck, dragged him to his feet, and led him hobbling out of the pen. Only actually perked up a little at this, thinking that perhaps they were about to let him go, but the man led the dogs around the back of a squat cinderblock building to a spot where there was an apparatus of some kind that looked like a large, green, front-loading washing machine. The man led the first two dogs, small terrier-like animals, up to the door, opened it and shoved them inside. Then he locked the door and turned on a valve on top of the machine and sat down on a bench, still holding Only and the other dog on the ropes. After about five minutes the man got up, turned the valve off and opened the door to the apparatus and stepped back for another minute or so, then reached in and hauled out the first two dogs. They lay limp, with lips curled back above their fangs in horrible grimaces. He lugged them by their tails to a big square metal bin with a brick chimney on top and tossed them inside, then came back for Only and his companion, an old toothless female mutt. The keeper seemed to take no pleasure at his task, but on the other hand he performed it dutifully, and Only did not like the look of this at all.

* * *

"George," Alice said, "I don't know. I called this number. It was a veterinarian, and he said he sent the dog to the pound about three weeks ago but kept the ad running. He said that they might have put it to sleep already, but that he would call over there and tell them to hold it if we got up there today."

"Today!" George said. "I can't get up there today."

Alice sighed. "I've got to pick up the girls at school and, well, I guess I could get somebody else to do that, but, well, isn't there any way you can get off and take a run up there? I know it's probably not him, but, then maybe it is. And I . . . I . . ." She started to choke up. "If it's not, I just don't think I could bear to see a dog that's going to be put to sleep and—"

"I will do it," George broke in. "Just give me the directions." It had suddenly struck him that if Alice went by herself she was going to bring that dog home whether it was Only or not. "I'll call you soon as I find out," he said.

Fourteen

∽∾∾

THE KEEPER AT THE POUND RETURNED TO THE BENCH where he had left Only and the other dog tied up. Slowly and deliberately he freed the rope ends and began leading them toward the strange green apparatus. Only felt a shiver of fear and he accidentally stumbled and when the man tugged at the rope he had to struggle hard to get to his feet. The other dog balked, too, and when they reached the apparatus the man, still holding the ropes, opened the door and dragged the female dog forward and shoved her into the hole. She balked again, and the man put down the end of Only's rope, stepping on it with his foot to hold it in place, while he shoved the other dog through the small door. Only, still a little weak and unsteady on his three legs, sat down where it was more comfortable.

Once the other dog was inside, the man peered in and apparently determined it was too small for Only's enormous body as well, and so he slammed the door shut and turned on the little valve on top. In order to do this he momentarily had to take his foot off of Only's rope, figuring Only wasn't going far on three legs anyway, but Only waited for his moment, just when the man's back was turned, and he scrambled up and loped around the side of the building as fast as his three legs would carry him. It wasn't all that fast, but fortunately when the man discovered he'd escaped he wasn't immediately sure where Only had gone, and this gave Only a lifesaving few seconds to hobble into some shrubbery and vanish behind it. He heard the keeper's footsteps pounding on the grass and heard even his deep breathing as he loped along the row of shrubs to a street, which he crossed without even watching for traffic, and was narrowly missed by a car. There was a little vine-enshrouded ravine on the other side of the road, and Only scrambled down into it and made his getaway into a wood at the far end of the gully.

"I don't know if it was him or not," George said into the phone, "because just as they were about to put him in the gas chamber he ran off."

"They couldn't find him?" Alice asked excitedly.

"The guy said he looked for about two hours but not a sign. But he's pretty hard to miss, so they figure they'll round him up sooner or later. I've told them to hold him if they get him again."

"Does it sound like Only?" she asked plaintively.

"Well, it's hard to tell," George said. "But there's something else. This dog's lost a leg. He got hit by a truck, and the vet said he had to take the leg off. Couldn't save it."

Alice gave a sympathetic whimper. "Oh, poor thing," she cried. "But was there anything else? Anything that might indicate it's him?"

"Nothing except the fact that he ran off when they least expected it," George declared solemnly.

Still following his morning-evening-sun route, Only slowly and painfully made his way south. There were many opportunities for twists, turns and errors, and he might have chosen the wrong way, but whether it was by instinct or by chance, he did not, and eventually, tired, hungry and bedraggled, he arrived at the outskirts of the big unpleasant part of the city. He recognized it immediately from the smells and the blustering honking traffic. Fur matted, aching and bone-weary, Only hobbled through the streets. Nothing looked familiar, and he spent the first night picking through garbage cans in the rear of a cafe. Next morning the sun shone, and a kind of sparkle came over the city, and the leaves on the occasional sidewalk trees were brilliant green.

As he was making his way past a narrow alley he caught a glimpse of a dark shape lying there, watching. His blood began to rise, for it was the big black dog that had attacked him before, motionless, staring at him with those same little yellow eyes. Only waited for it to lunge out and finish him. He knew he was no match for the big dog now. But he was prepared to take his medicine and slowed his crippled gait and eyed the dog warily.

But instead of pouncing on him, the black dog rose slowly to his feet and ambled out to the sidewalk in front of Only. As they met, the dog moved around to Only's side and began sniffing. Then he suddenly raised his head, and his eyes widened in a sign of recognition. The two of them looked at each other for a moment; then the other dog turned and stared out down the wide street and beyond it, as if he could see a thousand miles, and he stayed that way until Only continued on. When he had gone another block Only looked back, and the big dog was still standing there, sniffing at the wind and gazing into the sky.

He got lost several times, but eventually Only began to sense a certain familiarity to things. Nothing in particular, but there were some old smells and sights that had a ring of remembrance. Then he came to the park where he had spent his first night beneath a bench and eaten the hot dog from the trash basket. The bench was still there, but the basket was gone, and he went to sleep hungry, but a contentment settled over him like a warm blanket, for he knew he was close to the end of his journey. Sometime before dawn it began to rain, a sweet spring drizzle, and Only huddled under his bench and let the water fall softly on him. Just after first light he struggled to his feet and moved on. He spent several hours going through suburban neighborhoods. He remembered them vaguely and knew he was close. It rained most of the day, and in the afternoon he crossed a street and there, on the far side, was his old park, completely deserted, but the same as he had left it.

He wandered past the children's playground and the baseball diamond, inundated and muddy. He crossed a wide open field and hobbled through a stand of trees and went up the little slope to the street where he lived. He sat down on his haunches in the grass and stared at the house for a long time. No lights were on, and his heart began to pound, and a tremor of guilt ran through him. He would probably be punished and he wondered what form the punishment would take. He hated scolding. He hated the shrill authoritative voices of discipline when he had done something wrong, but somehow it didn't really matter now, because he missed them. He even missed the leash. He wanted to be home.

The light was fading, and the rain had stopped, and Only finally got up the courage to get to his feet and just before he crossed the street, he took one last backward look at the park below him, then blinked and craned his neck more. Even with his dimming eyesight, he could make out a shape down near the little stand of trees.

Standing stock-still, with her head raised toward him, was Blossom.

Only tensed, then quivered for an instant, then started toward her, negotiating the downward slope the best he could. He was embarrassed when he stumbled near the bottom and went rolling pell-mell for a few yards, but he regained his feet and hobbled as quickly as he could to where she stood frozen in the soft, wet grass.

He could see the man who owned her standing back in the trees, smoking a cigarette and looking absently in another direction. Only came to Blossom and sniffed, and she hunkered down slightly, then nosed up to him and bumped his shoulder. Her big liquid eyes stared into his face, and her tongue lapped out, and she investigated his stump of a hind leg. He noticed that she had gotten slightly gray around her muzzle but her coat was as fine and silky as it ever was, and he darted at her, watched her jump for joy and then he hobbled off, and she followed him, and they romped, the two of them, to the far end of the park, behind some shrubs. What they did there, for a few moments until Blossom's owner charged up and drove him away with shouts and hollering, was like a culmination of all the things Only existed for in his life. It was incomprehensible, mysterious and wonderful, the elusive high-water mark he had been seeking all these years but never found, and he knew it wouldn't really matter now whether he ever found it again. He watched from the distance, balanced on his three legs, as Blossom was led away into the twilight on her leash. All the pain and anguish and fear receded in Only. He waited until she was out of sight, then marched deliberately up the grassy slope and across the street to the quaint narrow old house where he'd been raised.

A light rain, almost a mist, had begun to fall again when Only reached the door. He stood on the brick sidewalk for a short while and looked up into the lighted windows. No face was to be seen, but he heard faint voices and laughter and squeals that he recognized as the girls', although they were older-sounding. Then he heard a male voice he instantly recognized as George's and a gay reply from a voice he knew was Alice's. He went to the door and with a pounding heart he raised his right front paw and scratched. It was the most difficult of maneuvers, since he had only three legs now and had to balance on his right rear and left front, and he nearly toppled over. But he managed to do it again, bracing his hind leg on some little bricks at the sidewalk edge. Nothing happened. He scratched once again, but the conversation inside continued undisturbed. He moved back out into the street and tried to see in the windows, but no human face was visible. Then he barked, his deep single "woof."

The conversation inside stopped. Alice's face appeared in the window, looked down at him, startled, then disappeared; then three other faces, George's and two girls', appeared, their noses pressed against the glass. Suddenly the front door burst open, and Alice rushed out hysterically, crying, "Oh, oh, oh . . ." and threw her arms around his neck, which toppled him over, and the two of them lay in a heap on the sidewalk until George strode out, followed by the girls, and all of them fell into the heap, hugging and touching and licking and crying, and Only was suddenly lifted into the air by George and carried ceremoniously into the house. Straining and grunting, George lugged Only up the stairs, through the old living room and into the little library with the fireplace and deposited him on the floor, where he promptly fell down because the wood was bare, and his paws had no purchase. They fussed over him so much that he began to feel embarrassed. He barely recognized the girls and he noticed that Alice had gone back to wearing the same kind of tidy clothes she had worn in his younger days. Other than that, nothing much had changed. When the pandemonium let up, Alice went to the kitchen and returned with a large bowl of human food, succulent meat of some kind, mixed with potatoes and a thick gravy. Only ate it greedily. He was the center of attention for the rest of the night. They catered to his every whim and even gave him a bowl of ice cream. Finally the girls were sent off to bed, and Alice and George sat in the little library talking happily, sipping from a bottle of wine, while Only lay in his old spot on the floor in front of the fireplace.

"I wish he could tell us where he's been," Alice said sweetly. "And what his experiences were."

"I wish he'd tell us why he left," George said.

"I think I know," she said.

"Maybe you were right."

"His fur's so matted," she said. "I'll get a brush tomorrow and untangle it. And his poor leg. He must have been so scared and hurt and lonely. . . ."

"I think he gave me a hernia," George said, "carrying him up those stairs."

Fifteen

〜〜〜

ONLY SETTLED EASILY BACK INTO LIFE IN WIMBELDON. Something deep inside told him he had finally come home for good. Alice and George looked a little older, but were more content with themselves than before he left. The girls, Kimberly and Caroline, were a joy, old enough now not to pull at his ears and stick their fingers in his eyes, and they were affectionate and warm.

The day after his return Only was let out into his garden and got both a shock and a rumple of delicious satisfaction.

The shock was that the garden had been rejuvenated and planted and trimmed to perfection; his excavations were filled and smoothed over, and grass was planted and mowed and the brick scrubbed. A bright spring sun beamed over freshly budding flowers and shrubs. Only ambled out and stood there for a long while surveying the scene. It wasn't the way he'd have done it, but then, he had to expect a few changes, he conceded.

He found a quiet sunny spot just along the side of the brick wall and sat down and after a while he was half-asleep with his head resting between his paws. Suddenly a shadow was cast in front of him from atop the wall. Only raised an eyebrow and remained absolutely motionless as the shadow moved stealthily along until it seemed to be just above him. The outline was unmistakable. It was the cat.

During the years of his departure, the cat had enjoyed virtual supremacy in the garden. It had lounged there, caught and killed birds, strolled across the cool grass with impunity. Obviously it had neither noticed him, nor gotten wind of his return.

Only stayed as still as a lion in high grass, watching the shadow of the cat as it casually licked its paws and flicked its tail. He had to stop himself from trembling in anticipation. The cat got up and arched its back, stretching, and as Only lay frozen, it coiled itself and leaped down into the garden, right in front of him.

Sometime in midleap it saw Only, but that split second of horrible realization was still not enough time for the cat to prepare itself for what was to come. Only slapped out with a paw and smacked the cat's tail down on the brick floor, pinning it. There was a flurry of screeching and turmoil as Only snapped out at the quivering tail and bit down on it and at the same time batted the cat's head with his other paw to keep it at bay. He was unable to rise quickly because of his missing leg, but that didn't matter. With a savage twist of his head he lifted the cat off the ground by its tail and at the apex of its ascension he let go and sent it flying through the air four or five feet.

The commotion raised by the cat was so horrible that anyone not actually witnessing the incident would have thought the cat was being murdered. Instead, it just wound up losing some fur. It hit the ground running and scrambled up a tree and bounded into a adjoining garden, wailing and shrieking. Only hadn't even gotten to his feet.

Finally! he thought. He spent the rest of the day savoring his coup with dark satisfaction. Finally.

As the days went by, Only fell into the old routine, but Alice was there most of the time, and the girls came home from school in the afternoon, and George got home at the usual time. He was taken to his park every day, unleashed, because he really couldn't go very fast on three legs. At least two or three times a week Blossom would be there, and they would walk together and sniff and smell and root. One day Blossom's owner came over to George, who was sitting on a bench, watching them.

"Well," he said with resignation, "I think your hound is about to become a father."

George looked up at him curiously. "What do you mean?"

"Well, about a month or so ago I caught old Only here in, uh, let's say a 'compromising position' with Blossom. It was the right time—or the wrong time, depending on how you look at it—but I took her to the vet's the other day and she's going to have a litter."

"No kidding," George said.

"No kidding," the man replied.

"Well, what do you suggest, a shotgun wedding perhaps?"

"He ought to assume some responsibility," the man said.

"Make an honest dog out of her?"

"Something like that."

"When is she due?"

"A few months," the man said.

"How do you know it was him?"

"Are you implying that my dog is promiscuous?"

"How would I know?" George said. "Morality has gone down the drain these days."

"I caught him in the act," the man said testily.

"Well, why don't we wait and see what the result is," said George. "I mean, if they come out looking like a bulldog or something, then he isn't the culprit—right?"

"That's true enough," the man conceded. "Be interesting to see what they're like though."

George nodded. Only was watching them from a

distance, sensing he was being discussed. George looked at him and shook his head. "I might have expected he'd get into something like this," he said sourly.

The next week Only was packed into the car, a new station wagon, and driven by Alice to the office of Dr. Peltz.

"It's amazing," the vet said as he examined Only. "How many years has it been?"

Old Dobie was delighted, and chucked Only under the chin.

The vet was looking at the stump of the leg. "The guy who did this did a pretty good job," he said. "Too bad the leg had to come off though. It's going to be a problem for him."

"How do you mean?" Alice said.

"Well, I haven't looked at the X rays yet, but from the feel of it, the other hip was dislocated at the same time. The guy relocated it, but there's going to be an awful lot of pressure on that hip now, and if it starts giving him trouble, it's going to be a problem. I'm just letting you know."

"You know, Doc," Dobie said, "I bet I can make a kind of wooden leg and fit it on him somehow. Take some of that pressure off."

Dr. Peltz shook his head. "Old dog like this—no way he'd learn to use something like that. Probably gnaw it off the first day. If he was younger . . ."

"I could give it a try," Dobie said.

The vet went to his cabinet and prepared a big needle for a rabies booster shot. "Never work," he said. "Dog's too old. Probably cause more trouble than it's worth." Only winced stoically as the doctor plunged the needle into him. Why was it that every time he got around these people they stuck him with needles? he wondered. Humans were really hard to figure out.

That spring drifted lazily into summer, and Only found himself more and more the center of attention of Caroline and little Kimberly. They invented a game where they would roll a tennis ball at him on the ground, and he would grab it in his mouth without having to get up, which, as Dr. Peltz had predicted, was becoming increasingly difficult. If the ball was rolled within reach of his mouth, and he caught it, both he and the roller got a point. If he failed to catch it, or if the roller rolled it out of his reach, each lost a point. They would do this for hours on end, with Only basking in the shade of his garden. On the refrigerator they kept a weekly scoreboard, and after six weeks Only was comfortably ahead by twenty-one points. Pretty good for an old fellow, who, by human standards, would be age sixty-three.

But the hip was becoming more and more painful. Some days, especially when it rained, Only had to be lifted to his feet.

He would let out a little "peep" and thrash around

a little, and if anyone was around they would pick him up gently by his hindquarters. Also he had problems urinating because he could not lift a leg, and the result was that he soiled his front legs and had to be washed a lot to keep him from smelling bad. It was undignified, and he knew it, but what else could he do?

One night George and Alice and the girls all went someplace and left the garden door open for Only, but it was one of those days when the hip was especially giving him a lot of trouble. When they got home they found that he had managed to drag himself across the floor with his front paws to the steps that led to the garden, where he had wanted to relieve himself. But he hadn't been able to get down the steps and had been in considerable discomfort and finally, involuntarily, "let go," wetting his fur and the floor too.

"Oh, poor thing," Alice said gently, as she lifted him up. "Poor thing."

George shook his head sadly and sighed. "It's going to be a rough winter for him," he said.

"Maybe we could make him a wheelchair," Alice said as she wiped up the wet spot on the floor.

George said nothing but went outside and stood in the garden, looking up at the stars. Only followed him out and stood beside him. George reached down and patted him on the head. "How'd you like some pot roast this Sunday?" he asked. "Would you like that?" Only lapped out with his tongue at

George's hand and gave a small wiggle of his back-side.

It wasn't too long after summer's end, when the first leaves began to turn and fall from the trees, and the sky became clear cool blue, and Only was lying in his garden, waiting for the cat (which, incidentally, had not shown itself at all since their last encounter), that he heard a great commotion inside the house. There were squeals of delight from the girls and Alice and a lot of talking and clamor. As the commotion got nearer, Only tried to struggle to his feet but sank back after a few tries. Then he saw them all standing in the doorway to the garden, George in front, followed by the girls and then Alice.

George had something in his arms, and Only squinted to see what it was. It was small and fluffy and auburn-colored and it squirmed. The procession stopped behind George at about the middle of the garden, and George bent down and placed the object on the ground. It moved unsteadily then spied Only and toddled over to him.

It was a tiny puppy, perhaps two months old. As it approached he thought he saw something vaguely familiar about it. Perhaps in its gait, or the way it carried its head, and as it neared there was something in its greenish eyes that reminded him of Blossom. It came right up to Only and nipped him on his nose.

Startled, Only drew back and batted the puppy with his big paw, sending it tumbling. George went

over and scooped the puppy up, and Alice helped
Only to his feet.

"That was some introduction," George said.

"They'll get along fine," Alice said.

George put the puppy down again, and Only
hobbled over to it and nosed it, and it licked his
snout.

"I can't get over how beautiful he is," Alice said.

"Just like America, I guess," George observed.
"No pure breeds much anymore, but when you mix
up the melting pot, Germans marrying Italians,
Spaniards marrying Swedes and so on, you sometimes get remarkable results."

"Yes," Alice purred, "just like America. An 'All-
American' dog."

"What are we going to call him?" Caroline asked.

"Why not call him America?" Alice said.

"America?" George winced. "What kind of name
is that?"

"About the same as 'Only,'" Alice said.

"That's what I mean," George said. "Why can't
we call him Fido? Keep it simple."

"*America,*" Alice said soothingly.

And so it was.

It took Only about three days to realize that
America was actually his replacement. At first he
wasn't sure whether the puppy was just there for a
visit or to stay, but on the third day it suddenly
dawned on him that George had a greater plan in

mind when he brought the puppy home. Caroline and Kimberly fawned over America as though he were a precious jewel. For a week or so, Only sulked and remained listless at this thunder-stealing, but then he made a decision. If this was the way it was to be, it was the way it *would* be, and he contributed as best he could by communicating to America the lessons he had learned himself as a puppy. He growled at him when he caught him doing his business inside the house. He grunted in disapproval if America began to tear up paper and strew it on the floor or gnaw on furniture. He cuddled with him at night to keep him from whimpering. He was both mother and father and after a while he began to enjoy the role.

Autumn became winter, and it was particularly bleak and foul. Only's hip problem was exacerbated, and it finally got to the point where he could barely get to his feet at all.

In the spring the rains made it even worse, and to aggravate things further he caught the flu or something like it and was weakened and helpless day after day. It humiliated him, having to be tended to for even the meagerest need or want: helped to his feet, assisted outside to do his business. The virus laid him so low that he no longer could get to the park and suffered the additional indignity of having to relieve his bowels in his own garden. During those weeks time became a swirl of memories, some happy, some bitter, some sweet and some sad. He thought back fondly of Jake, who was put into the cold ground, and of Elsie. He remembered the big vicious dog in the city who attacked him and who, on his return, had accorded him a proper recognition. In his dreams he recollected the sheep and carrying the newspapers up to people's front porches countless times and killing and eating the duck. Occasionally nightmares would bring back the ordeal in the ocean and being hit by the truck. But his fondest memories were reserved for Blossom, and whether they were conscious recollections or the product of his dreams, a warmth and hope and sense of peace would come over Only whenever he thought of her. Even though he could not see her anymore, she lived in his consciousness through America, who was growing big and strong and fine.

By summer, Only was beginning to recover from the illness but still felt weakened and despondent. It had rained heavily the day before, and that night Only could hear George and Alice talking quietly about him, almost in whispers. Next morning the rain continued, but Only was helped up by Alice, who got him into the station wagon and drove him to Dr. Peltz's office. Oh no, he thought, here I go again.

Dobie lifted him onto the steel examining table, and the vet prodded and looked while Dobie stroked his head and Alice stood by watching. There were no shots this time, and when Dr. Peltz was finished he sighed and walked out into the hall with Alice while

Dobie continued to rub Only behind the ears and talked soothingly to him.

When Alice returned, Only noticed that her eyes were filled with tears, and she went to him and petted him gently and put her hand under his chin and raised his head, and then she put her cheek next to his, and he licked it. Dobie and the vet carefully lifted Only off the table and put him on the floor, and he followed Alice slowly out to the car. He sat in the front seat next to her on the ride home, looking out of the window. Every once in a while she would look over at him and touch him. He wondered what she was upset about and wished that he could help her.

Sixteen

✤

WHEN GEORGE CAME HOME THAT NIGHT THERE WAS A family meeting of sorts. First Alice and George went into the library and talked in monotones. Alice said something about "just a few more days," but Only could hear George saying, "Look, if it's got to be done, it's better to get it over with. It'll just make it worse to drag it out."

When the girls came home both George and Alice went up to their room before supper, and there was another conversation there, and when they all came down, the girls ran to Only and threw their arms around him.

Alice was cooking supper and soon the smell of steak wafted through the house. The mood at the dinner table was somber, but Only was helped into the dining room and a large platter was set before him containing an enormous piece of cut-up steak, the most delicious meal he had ever had, and he gobbled it up greedily. America sat solemnly in a corner with his head resting between his paws. Earlier he had been scolded for getting muddy paws on the sofa.

The family sat together for a long time that night, talking quietly, and Only received an unusual amount of affection; more even than when he had first returned home. After the girls had gone to bed George and Alice remained with Only lying at their feet. They had finished one bottle of wine and were about to finish another.

"All these years," Alice said lovingly. She rubbed Only's back with her toe.

"I guess he wasn't retarded after all," George said. "Crazy maybe, but not retarded."

"I don't know if I can go through with it," she said, gulping down another glass of wine.

"It's better, babe," George said. "I know what you mean. But he's suffering. Peltz wouldn't have made his prognosis otherwise."

She lowered her head to George's shoulder and sighed. "We'll be there with him," she said. "All the time."

"I don't know about that," George said. "Let's see what Peltz says is best."

Next morning was a glorious sunny summer day; bees hummed and butterflies fluttered in Only's garden. He was sleeping under a shrub when something woke him, and he opened one eye to catch a glimpse of the cat on the wall, staring at him. He raised his head and stared back, and after a minute or two the cat disappeared into its own yard. A thick rich aroma of food was lifted from the kitchen and was carried on a summer's breeze into the garden. It was pot roast, and Only perked up. This wasn't Sunday, he knew that, because they had just had a Sunday with pot roast a few days before. His mind felt clouded, and he tried to clear his memory. Perhaps he was wrong. But it was unmistakably pot roast.

But the girls were home and dressed and they came out into the garden, followed by America, and began playing the ball-rolling game with Only. They had added a new twist since America's arrival. If he could intercept the ball on its course to Only, America got a point too. Nevertheless, Only maintained a comfortable lead.

The morning seemed to pass slowly. George and Alice sat in the garden around a little table, talking casually. Only noticed that they both had fixed themselves glasses of whiskey and refilled them several times. Late in the afternoon, cool shadows had crept across the garden floor, and George got up and went inside. His voice could be heard talking on the phone, then he reappeared in the garden doorway, and Alice had a look of cold, tense horror in her face. George nodded. "Let's go, girls," he said. "You get America." He went over to Only and lifted him to his feet. "Come on, old boy," he said. "We have to go now."

George drove, and the girls were in the back seat, and America was in the rear. Only was let into the front seat and allowed to lie on the floor like he had when he was a puppy, cooled by the little air vent. When Alice got in she had a large pan with her, filled with the wonderful-smelling pot roast. As they drove off, she put it down in front of Only, and he lapped at the thick gravy and chewed the meat and vegetables. Not a word was said all the way to Dr. Peltz's office.

When they pulled into the parking lot, George got out and opened the door for Alice, and she helped Only out onto the hot concrete. The girls got out, too, and Only nosed up to them. They seemed visibly upset, but were not crying. They hugged him and kissed him for a while, until George said, "I think you'd better get back in the car now." That was when they began to cry, but they did as they were told. Only looked up at the rear window. America was standing there with his nose pressed against it, and he let out a deep lone "woof."

George and Alice led Only into Dr. Peltz's office. Inside there were perhaps half-a-dozen people sitting there: women with cats on their laps, several dogs and a sour-looking old man with an enormous-beaked bird in a cage. Only gave the bird the kind of condescending glance that humans might reserve for a monkey in a zoo. At least, Only thought, *he* didn't have to be kept in a cage.

Only hobbled dutifully past these other creatures, up to a pretty girl in a white uniform who was seated at a reception desk. Words were said, and the girl came from behind the desk and slipped a rope over Only's head and petted him. Alice knelt down and threw her arms around Only's neck and began to cry softly. George knelt down, too, and the three of them stayed that way for a while. The pretty girl in the white uniform waited patiently, seeming a little embarrassed, but she said nothing. Dobie appeared from a hallway and began talking to Only in his strange, hyperactive tone. George got up, but Alice remained kneeling.

"We'd better go now, babe," he said.

She was biting her lip. "Oh George, can't we stay with him? I know what the vet said, but don't you think . . ."

George shook his head. "It just isn't a good idea," he said. "The vet has been through this before, and I think we ought to trust his judgment."

Her eyes brimmed with tears as she tore herself away from Only, who looked up at her curiously, not understanding what all the fuss was over.

"I'm sorry, Mrs. Martin," Dobie said. "We'll treat him real good though. It won't be bad on him at all."

She looked down at Only then bent down once more and kissed him on his big, black, damp nose.

George turned to Dobie. "We'll be back in the morning, then," he said. "You'll have everything ready?"

"Yessir," Dobie said. George reached down and patted the furry bewildered head. He tried to say something, but the words caught in his throat. He tried to clear it, and then wiped his eyes with his sleeve and followed Alice out the door. The girl in the white uniform handed the rope to Dobie, who led Only into the examining room, where Dr. Peltz was waiting.

"I don't like this one at all, Doc," Dobie said. "I put down a lot of animals with you, but I got a bad feelin'. Real bad. This dog is *people.*"

"I don't like it either," Peltz grumbled, "but what can you do? It's the worst part of this work." He went to the cabinet and took out a very large needle. "Get him up on the table, Dobie," the vet said.

Suddenly a great commotion broke out in the waiting room, a lot of growling and snarling. "Oh hell Dobie," Peltz said, "go see what that's all about and then come on back." Dobie vanished through the door. Only gazed out of a low window in time to see the station wagon pass by. In the back seat the girls' faces were peering out the window, and he could see the lion-like mane of America staring at the building as the car pulled away into the street. Dr. Peltz was fumbling with a vial of something that he had taken from a locked glass cabinet and then doing something with the needle. It was the biggest, scariest needle Only had ever seen, and he winced at the thought of getting stuck with it. He just didn't like that idea at all. He took a stealthy hobbled step toward the open door and then another while Peltz, his back turned toward him, filled the needle from the vial.

Dr. Peltz had raised the needle high into the air when Only sneaked out into the hall. It was empty. Through another door he heard Dobie trying to quiet down two quarreling dogs. He decided to try the far end of the hallway, and he loped along the plastic tile until he came to a large room with a screen door that led to an open area. He nosed open the door and hobbled down some steps into the warm afternoon.

There was a big field overgrown with grass and brambles that began where Peltz's parking lot ended, and Only loped into it. He hadn't gone far when he heard a shout. Glancing back, he saw Dr. Peltz, standing on the steps in his white smock, hollering at him. Only stopped for a moment and looked at him. Suddenly Dobie's face appeared in the door and behind him the girl from the reception desk. Peltz took off, running toward Only, followed by the other two. "Fan out!" he shouted.

Only ran as fast as he was able, but they were gaining on him. Then he ran smack into a tall wire-link fence. He ran along the fence for a while until he saw that it ended with another fence—a dead end. He ran back, but he could see Peltz and the nurse coming at him. Dobie had fanned out and was circling around behind him. Only came to a halt, trying to figure out what his next move was. He realized he wasn't fast enough anymore to escape them. Peltz was only a few yards away when Only saw a small hole under the fence. It was his last chance, and he scrambled for it. Sharp wire from the hole snagged in his fur, and for a moment he was caught. Peltz was grabbing for him when he pulled himself free and bolted loose. There were oaths and much shouting from the opposite side of the fence.

Only found himself in a strange place, a big yard with cinders and rails. He trotted a little way toward a line of freight cars parked on the tracks.

"Dobie, see if you can get under that fence and get him," Peltz cried. The nurse and the vet ran alongside Only on their side of the fence while Dobie tried to wriggle beneath it. Only stopped and lifted his head, for he had caught a whiff of something that registered in his brain, some long ago smell of damp hay, reminding him of the chicken coop back in the village and even further back than that, of something in his early life of cows and security. He followed the smell until he came on a car with open doors where the smell of the hay was coming from. Dobie had gotten through the fence and was bearing down on him. A screech came from the tracks by the freight car, and the monstrous steel wheels of the train lurched forward a few feet. Only stood in front of the opening of the car and gathered his strength, then sprang with all his might off his one good hind leg. He got his front paws on the floor of the cattle car, but it was nearly four feet off the ground, and he slid back down. Again he mustered all his might and leaped up, but this time he banged his nose on the edge of the car and fell in a heap on the cinders. He was scrambling up for another try when Dobie collared him.

"Good, Dobie!" Dr. Peltz shouted from behind the fence. "Get that rope tight—God forbid we should lose him!" The train lurched again.

"Right, Doc," Dobie said.

But suddenly Only felt himself being hoisted into the air and deposited feet first into the soft hay of the boxcar. Befuddled, he looked down at Dobie, who was facing Dr. Peltz defiantly.

"Dobie, what on earth!" the vet shouted. "What do you think you're doing!"

"I'll tell you what I'm doin', Doc," Dobie cried. "I ain't going to do this. I put down a lot of animals, but I ain't puttin' down this one. Not while he's got this kind of steam left in him. Mercy, he ain't no worse off than me. I suppose you'd put me down, too, wouldn't you!"

"Dobie, are you crazy?" Peltz roared. "Get him out of there before the train pulls off!"

"I reckon I *am* crazy, Doc." Dobie said. "Everybody thinks I am anyway. So what! Hell, I always wanted to see the country anyhow. Looks like this is my chance!" He put a foot on an iron rung and clambered aboard the train, which gave a final lurch, then began to roll out of the yard.

"Dobie!" Dr. Peltz screamed. "You're out of your mind!"

"I know it!" Dobie cackled back. "Ain't it grand!"

The train began to pick up speed, and Only stuck his head out of the door. He glanced at the orange August sun setting behind a bank of scarlet clouds. Looking back, he could see the diminishing figures of Dr. Peltz, standing with his hands on his hips, and beside him, the pretty girl from the reception desk. Just as the train rounded a curve she raised her hand in a tentative little flutter, like a wave.

He blinked into the distance once or twice as the train headed west, toward places he had never seen.

Epilogue

～～～～

"**I** CHECKED WITH THE DISPATCHER IN THE RAILROAD yard," Dr. Peltz was saying apologetically into the phone. "That train's headed for California. We could get them picked up any number of places along the way."

"I don't think so," George said. "Something just tells me this time to leave things the way they are."

"If it's any consolation," Peltz said, "I don't suppose either of them is going to last very long."

"In a way I guess I'm relieved," George said. "I just don't see how he did it, though."

"Mr. Martin," Dr. Peltz said, "nothing I've ever been involved with concerning that dog has ever been normal. He's just plain obstinate."

"That he is," George said. "That he is."

By sunup the train had reached Illinois and was rocking along through fields of grain, past little towns and abandoned depots.

Only was sitting in a pile of the sweet-smelling straw, and Dobie was in a corner with his back against the wall of the boxcar, whittling away with a penknife on a plank of two-by-four he had found in the car.

"Yep," he said, "gonna fit this ole wood leg on you and make you good as new. You'll prob'ly look like some old pirate. Ought to get a bird and put it on your shoulder and a patch over your eye too. I'm gonna paint this leg red, white and blue. Who knows, we get to California, maybe we even get on the Johnny Carson show."

At this, Only's ears perked up.

"I wonder where they are now, and what they're doing," Alice said. They were sitting in the living room on a wintry Saturday afternoon. George had his feet propped up on a coffee table, reading the paper. He put it down. "Knowing Only," he said, "he'll probably wind up in the movies. Be a big star like Lassie or Rin Tin Tin or something."

Alice looked out of the window and suddenly jumped to her feet and ran to the door to the garden. "My God," she said. "George, come look at this!"

George got up and looked out the door. Alone in the back of the garden was America. He had excavated an enormous hole in the ground and was standing and looking at them with an indescribably filthy snout and paws. A mixture of guilt and defiance was etched in his face.

"Just like his father," Alice said tenderly.

"Greatgodamighty," George moaned.

"Eureka!" Alice shouted.